Praise for Candy Caine

BECAUSE OF YOU "...Engrossing...a page turner... I would recommend this book!" — Romance Novels in Color "A sweet romance. I love the heartwarming ending." — Library Thing

FLAVOR OF THE WEEK "Pure light-hearted fun. A really heart-warming read with endearing characters." — LBAS Book Blog

FOR YOUR LOVE "...A cast of well-crafted characters you'll want to cheer for...delightful story..." — Niambi Brown Davis, Author of Sanctuary "A sexy, fabulous read. I couldn't put it down." — Bertrice Small, New York Times bestselling author

MORE HEATED PLEASURES "...Candy Caine once again hits the right erotic sweet spots..." — Cynthia White, author of Awakened Desire "A roller coaster ride of erotic thrills... Great fun!" — Alice Gaylord, author of The Reluctant Handyman

NO STRINGS ATTACHED "Good quick read with sex, secrets, and trauma." — Reading By The Book

SAVE THE LAST DANCE FOR ME "A story about real relationships...the romance between Evie and Dillon is electric. Candy Caine's writing is impressive." — Latrivia S. Nelson, bestselling author of The Ugly Girlfriend

Candy Caine's tribute to the power of love is showcased in the following stories...

A Golden Matchmaker

After breaking up with Haywood Lewis, Kendra Robinson had begun to feel awful and doubt the wisdom of the move, though her reasons for doing so had been sound. She had the inkling that he was using her for sex and might be cheating, as well. Still having to eat, Kendra goes to the supermarket. Heading to her car, she chases away boys terrorizing a Golden Retriever named Gus. Kendra calls the dog's owner, Duncan Green. To thank Kendra, Duncan takes her out to dinner, but even though he's nice and easy on the eyes, Kendra fears rushing into anything on the rebound. And despite all that, Haywood isn't ready to let Kendra go.

All You Need is Love

Jenny Smith worries that if she doesn't take better control of her life and find a guy to marry and have a family, she'll end up all alone with only her nursing career. She signs up on an online dating site and has a horrible first date. Her luck changes when she goes on a blind date to help out a friend. However, she later learns that her online date could have turned out differently.

A Christmas Present to Remember

When Michelle Madsen receives a phone call from a woman representing herself as her father's wife, it turns her life upside down.

Beneath the Velvet Blue Moon

During the summer of her 19th year, Nadine Stone falls in love with Michael Greene. However, when a family tragedy strikes, she loses contact with him and in time moves on. Eventually, she meets another terrific guy, but when he proposes to her, she senses something is missing from their relationship. Needing to sort things out, Nadine heads back to the place she used to vacation with her parents, the same one she'd met Michael Greene, and realizes what is missing.

When the Hearts Errs

Sandra Kramer meets Richard James at the cemetery, the day she buries her mother. At first, he's a comfort, but soon they begin to date. Six months later, he proposes and promises to love her forever. Only Sandra's beautiful world begins to unravel when Richard goes on a business trip.

Icecapade

One of the outdated laws still on the books in Newcastle, Wyoming prohibits fornication standing up in a walk-in freezer. When MaryAnnHedges sells an article to a magazine, she wants to celebrate with a pork chop dinner. Only when she asks for just one, the butcher at Smith's Meats, Jake Bronson, confronts her. "No one buys only one." This leads to a heated argument and the end result is that Jake goes to her place to cook two pork chops. They end up dating and falling in love. However, when MaryAnn discovers that Jake has a gambling problem like her dad, she threatens to break up with him. He promises to stop gambling, but he lapses and they find themselves hiding from his bookie in a meat freezer. The bookie trashes the store and what happens next is a crime.

ALL YOU NEED IS LOVE
A Collection of Short Stories
By Candy Caine

All names, characters, and incidents featured in this publication are imaginary. Any resemblance to actual persons (living or dead) is coincidental. They are not inspired even distantly by any individual or incident known or unknown to the author.

Author recognizes that all trademarked items mentioned in the book belong to the trademark holders of said items.

Table of Contents

A GOLDEN MATCHMAKER

The alarm went off. I opened one eye, reached over...and knocked the darn clock to the floor. The noise of the buzzer was echoing in my head as I bent over the side of the bed to retrieve it. I felt so out of sorts and lay back down on my pillow again. All at once, I remembered why.

Haywood and I were supposed to go to dinner and a movie. He had called and said he'd be late. A last-minute client had wanted to see an apartment. Lately, he had been getting an unusual number of last-minute people and it was nearly 9:00 pm when he finally arrived. I was no longer hungry.

He walked into my apartment as if nothing was wrong. I was angry, but it wasn't only because he was late again, but compounded by the fact our relationship appeared to be going nowhere.

Haywood tried to take me in his arms, but I backed away.

"What?"

"Is this all I mean to you?"

"A guy ain't supposed to kiss his girl hello?"

I shook my head. "That's not it."

He looked at me as if I were crazy. "What's gotten into that head of yours? Are you mad 'cause I'm late again?"

"No...yes—but it's only a small part."

"A small part of what?" He asked, raising an eyebrow.

I knew that look. He was getting mad. "Yeah, you're late again. No dinner—"

"If you're hungry, I'll take you to get something to eat."

"I'm not hungry!" I blurted out, frustrated.

"Then *what* is it?"

"We never go out anywhere. All we do is have sex."

"What's wrong with sex?"

"Everything if that's all I mean to you," I replied with a hint of anger in my voice.

"Girl, you know that's not true."

"Do I? We've been together for over a year and our relationship appears to be going nowhere."

"Where do you—hey! I see where this conversation is going, but I'm not heading that way, he spat, eyes narrowing."

I could feel tears of pain and anger forming in my eyes.

"I'm just not ready now, baby, for marriage and having kids."

"When, then?"

He shrugged and gestured, "I gotta be free."

"Perhaps we both should have our freedom," I heard slip from my lips almost involuntarily.

"*Maybe you're right*," he said, anger clinging to every word.

Things escalated quickly from there. "Fine. Take what belongs to you and go," I said, running into the bathroom and slamming the door. By the time I came out ten minutes later, Haywood was gone.

I had cried myself to sleep. Perhaps I had been too hasty. Maybe I should have weaned myself from him rather than going cold turkey. I had been so miserable last night. Now, as I stepped into the shower, I wondered if all the tears were worth it.

Usually, a hot shower perked me up, but today it didn't. My hair didn't cooperate, either. I was late getting out of the house and the traffic was the pits. When I arrived at work ten minutes late, my supervisor, Josey, was at my station waiting for me. The look in her eyes sent shivers down my spine. Something told me I should have stayed in bed and called in sick.

"You're late, Kendra," she said as if I didn't already know.

"Traffic was terrible."

"You should have allowed for that by giving yourself extra time."

I felt a sarcastic answer rising in my throat and fought to keep my mouth shut. Everyone probably had their ears glued to the walls of their cubicles waiting for a good show. Fortunately for me, my fellow telemarketers weren't going to get one because Josey marched me into her small office.

"I'm going to make this quick. I have to let you go, Kendra. Your productivity has been down lately—"

"Fine. I'm history. What else could possibly go wrong today?" I thought to myself.

"Accounting has your last check. I wish you luck."

"That seems to be something I've been short of lately," I muttered and left her office.

When I reached my car in the parking lot, it appeared to lean to one side. Then I saw the nail protruding from my rear tire. I had a flat tire, no job, and a huge headache.

After I had my tire fixed, I stopped at the supermarket to pick up a few things. I ended up adding to my miserable day by getting on a line from Hell. By the time I left, food in hand, the pain in my head was doing a tap dance between my ears.

As I carried the packages from my car to my apartment, I was nearly knocked down by a dog running from some kids on bikes. They appeared to be terrorizing the poor animal.

"Hey! Leave that dog alone!"

"Why?" a tall, pimply-faced, kid asked. "He yours?" He was challenging me.

"Yeah. Here, boy!" I called to the frightened dog. He came racing back and hid behind my legs.

That seemed to convince them and they rode off having their fun spoiled. I looked at the large yellow dog that was furiously wagging his tail against my legs. He was probably thirsty.

"Come on, fella," I said walking to the door.

After I put the packages down, I poured some water into a bowl.

He quickly drank that bowl and the next two. I put away my groceries. The dog walked over to me and began to lick my hand.

"You're a friendly guy, aren't you," I said, checking out the tags on his collar.

One bone-shaped tag read: "I'm Gus. Please return me to Duncan. Call 467-4788."

"Okay, Gus, I guess I should call your owner. He must be worried sick about you."

I dialed the number and got an answering machine. I left a brief message and then shared some dinner with Gus.

"Your master has a pleasant-sounding voice. I'm sure he'll come for you soon."

I went outside with the dog so he could do his business. By the time we returned, there was a message on my answering machine from Duncan. It seemed that we were playing phone tag. I immediately called him back, half-expecting him to be elsewhere, but he picked up on the first ring.

"Are you the lady who found Gus?"

"Yes."

"He's all right? I was worried sick. I feared he ended up in the pound or had gotten hurt."

"Oh, he's fine."

"I'll come and get him. Where do you live?"

I imagined him to be tall and handsome. A short, fat man had no right to possess a wonderful voice like his. After giving him directions to my place, I barely had time to clean up the kitchen and make a pot of coffee before I heard my doorbell.

Gus barked and together we opened the door to a tall, attractive man with the most beautiful green eyes. His smile was wide and infectious. He held a leather leash in his hand. Gus immediately rushed the guy nearly knocking him over.

"Yes, I missed you, too, boy. That's a good boy. Glad to see you, too."

When he could catch his breath from the energetic greeting Gus had given him, I said, "I made a fresh pot of coffee. Would you like a cup?"

"Please forgive my manners. I'm Duncan Green and I'd love a cup."

I smiled, watching Gus and Duncan together. "I'm Kendra Robinson."

He followed Gus into my kitchen. I couldn't help but notice how he moved with such easy grace in the faded pair of jeans he wore that fit him like a glove. I could feel my body react to the sight as well.

"You have no idea how grateful I am. Gus found a hole in the fence and decided to go exploring."

"He obviously got lost. Luckily, he found me, because I had to save him from some nasty boys. He's such a love."

"That he is and way too trusting. Aren't you, fella," he said and ruffled his fur."

"I guess he's not a very good watchdog."

Duncan shook his head. "Golden Retrievers are notoriously affectionate and Gus is a prime example."

"I know from how he interacted with me. He's such a sweet dog."

Over the second cup of coffee, I learned more about Duncan. He was a divorce lawyer and single.

"Your being single has a silver lining. You won't ever need the services of a divorce lawyer."

Duncan chuckled. "And what do you do?"

"To be honest, I lost my job today. I had been a telemarketer, but perhaps it's time to look for another career, just the same."

"What would you like to do?" Duncan asked as Gus nudged him with his nose. For attention. He scratched behind the dog's ears.

"I hadn't decided."

"Can you type?"

"Yes."

"Would you be interested in becoming a secretary?"

"It's a thought. I can be flexible," I replied.

"I think I have just the job for you—Oh, no, not for me. It's for another lawyer whose secretary is moving out of state. Why don't you apply for the job?"

"I have nothing else... I guess I could."

"Great! I'll let Elaine know you'll be stopping by. She's our human resources manager. I know she'll love you. Got a pen and paper? I'll jot down all the particulars."

"This is so nice of you, Duncan," I said, as I got up and retrieved something to write on.

"That's only one of the things I intend to do for you."

"Oh? What's the other? You don't have to pay me or anything like that."

"No," he chuckled, "nothing like that. I just want to take you out for the best steak dinner you've ever had. That is if you're not a vegetarian."

"No. I happen to like steak. Vegetables are good as a side dish."

"Good. I'll pick you up at 7:00 on Saturday."

We talked a little more before Duncan took Gus home. I enjoyed being with him, but the best thing was that since I found Gus and met Duncan, I hadn't given one thought to Haywood. Of course, I feared that I had met Duncan too soon after Haywood and on the rebound. Even though he intrigued me, being so different from most of the men I had dated, I had to be careful and not rush into anything. Then there was the chance that Duncan was merely repaying me for my kindness with the steak dinner and not interested in dating me at all. I secretly hoped that wasn't the case.

Haywood hardly ever took me to fancy restaurants. It wasn't because he didn't have the money, because he made good commissions on his real estate deals. It was because he was a penny-pincher. How could I have been so low maintenance to accept it?

The restaurant that Duncan took me to was something else. It was so expensive; I thought the use of the bathrooms would be itemized into the tab. But the service and food were truly excellent, and the décor was in warm dark wood and supple leather to match.

There was a small dance floor and Duncan and I got up to dance.

"If you show up at the interview looking like you do tonight, the other lawyers will fire their secretaries. You look terrific."

"Thank you." I knew I was attractive with a fairly nice figure, but no femme fatale. I loved hearing him say it, though. It had taken me hours to select a red dress to wear with matching heels. To finish it off, I swept my dark hair up into a stylish look I borrowed from a picture in Cosmopolitan magazine. I also spent an inordinate amount of time on my makeup so that my hazel eyes popped.

When he took me in his arms and held me close, a sudden surge of warmth shot directly to my core. I blamed it on the wine and the excitement of the evening. But when he began to move against me, I could hardly mistake the desire he was arousing in me as well as himself.

"Take it slowly," my inner voice was whispering to me. "Don't rush into bed with him." Unfortunately, by the time we arrived back at my apartment, my hormones had drowned out that voice of reason. I quickly discovered that I desired this man more than I needed to take the next breath.

"Would you like to come in for a drink?"

His eyes shone as he said, "More than ever. I was hoping you'd ask."

As the door closed behind us, his lips covered mine. The kiss was gentle, almost playful. He looked into my eyes and smiled. The next kiss stole my breath away.

"Now I know how your lips taste. I need to taste the rest of you," he murmured into my neck before he kissed it.

I bent my head back, allowing him more access. As his lips caressed my neck, his fingertips teased my breast. My nipples grew hard and strained against the material of my dress, begging to be released.

He slowly unzipped my dress slipping his hand down my back, searing the flesh as he touched it. Feeling wanton, I stood up and let my dress fall to the floor and stepped out of it, unclasping my bra and allowing it to join my dress before I reentered his waiting arms.

Smiling, he lowered his lips to my breast and teased the nipple. I was so wet with desire that I pressed my body against his.

Duncan continued to arouse and excite me, bringing me closer to my sweet release. I unzipped his slacks and freed his straining erection. He let out a moan as I stroked it. A moment later, he had taken off the rest of his clothing. The feeling of his hot flesh on mine excited me even more.

He sensed I was more than ready and entered me slowly. As Duncan moved, move he let out another moan of pleasure, letting me know he was close to coming as well. It was a short, sweet ride to heaven for us both.

In the aftermath of our lovemaking, as we lay together, Duncan apologized to me.

"Kendra, I want to tell you something."

"Umm..." It was hard to concentrate on what he was saying while he absentmindedly stroked my nipple with a fingertip.

"I didn't mean for this to happen. I mean...I didn't set out to seduce you."

"No? How come? I'd like to think that I was the hottest, sexiest woman in the world."

"That you are."

"Sorry, I'm yanking your chain when I sense you want to be serious. To be honest, I had wanted to take things slow as well. After all, I'm rebounding from a relationship. But I'm far from sorry it happened."

"What happened between us was dynamite."

"I know. I felt it, too."

"Good," he said, as he rolled on top of me and started to devour my lips.

The day I had the interview, I didn't see Duncan, who was in court. Because of his glowing recommendations, and I'd like to think my qualifications, I was practically hired on the spot. I had to return to meet Alex James, the lawyer I'd be working for. I met him the next day and was hired. He was such a sweet guy, tall and nerdy looking. Duncan had mentioned to him that we were dating and he told me that he was envious. I hoped he was kidding, of course.

As the weeks passed, I discovered I truly liked working for Alex James. He was in court most of the time, so I ran things for him. We became good friends as well. The biggest fringe benefit, other than medical and dental coverage, was being able to have lunch often with the man who had stolen my heart. No matter how much I saw Duncan, I always seemed to want him more. I had tossed my caution to the wind and silenced that little voice of reason. I was Duncan's for the asking.

I hardly gave Haywood Lewis a thought until Duncan and I inadvertently bumped into him and his date at the movies one night. I tried to make believe that I hadn't seen him, but he came over and introduced the woman to us.

Duncan, sensing my discomfort, excused us quickly. As we walked away, he said, "So that was your ex."

"Keep any snide comments that you have to yourself."

He gave me a look. "He looked fairly decent. It was his date who needed a lot of help. A makeover, I believe they call it."

I chuckled. It was a nice way of calling her a dog. He did have a way with words.

"I guess it proves that you're one of a kind and cannot be duplicated," he said as he pulled me close and kissed me.

That night as Duncan was making sweet love to me the phone rang. Nothing could be that important that couldn't wait, so I allowed my answering machine to pick up. It wasn't until much later that I remembered to check for messages.

The voice was slurred, thick with drink, but unmistakably Haywood's. All he said was, "You'll never be free of me," but it unnerved me.

"Is that the guy we bumped into at the movies?"

"Uh-huh," I said, as an involuntary chill ran down my spine.

"A real homeboy."

I wasn't actually listening. Instead, I was thinking about what Haywood had said. Was he serious or just drunk? I didn't need this.

"Kendra? Are you alright? You're white as a ghost." Duncan asked, breaking into my thoughts.

"A little worried, that's all."

"Is he capable of becoming a problem?"

"I...I don't really know."

"Well, I'm here now, so he'd better stay away if he knows what's best," he said, putting a protective arm around my shoulders.

The days passed, but Haywood hadn't made good on his promise. Unfortunately, that didn't stop me from looking over my shoulder or listening for that knock at the door, though.

One evening Duncan walked into my apartment looking like the weight of the world was just dumped on his shoulders. He collapsed into a chair.

"My mother needs a quadruple bypass."

"Oh, dear," I said, walking behind his chair and hugging him, "I'm so sorry to hear that."

"The doctor assured me that the operation was practically routine. They'll have her up and walking the next day."

"When are you flying to Atlanta?"

"Tomorrow morning. The operation's the next day."

"I'll take you to the airport and pick you up when you're ready to come home. My prayers will go with you."

"I know that," he said, giving me a weak smile.

That night as I held him close, as I sensed he was wracked with worry. No matter what the doctor said, he feared something would go wrong. I wanted to possess the power to kiss all his fears away.

Duncan called me every day to let me know how his mother was doing. Unfortunately, I couldn't hold and kiss him through the phone wires. His mother had come through the operation fine and was doing better than the doctors expected. Five days after the procedure she was discharged from the hospital. A visiting nurse would stop by for the following week to make sure that she exercised her breathing correctly and took her medicine.

Duncan wasn't worried since his sister, Debbie, lived right down the block. He knew his mother would be looked after properly so he called to let me know that he was coming home the following night.

The next day dragged on. Concentrating on my work was out of the question. When I got home, I made dinner for myself and fed Gus who I was caring for while Duncan was away. He was good company and I was glad he was there with me.

I was about to call the airlines and check on Duncan's flight when a news bulletin came on the television. "Flight 362 from Atlanta had crashed right after takes off. No survivors. Details to follow on the ten o'clock news."

"No! No! No!" I screamed. "This can't be happening!"

Gus jumped up and nearly knocked me down. I grabbed him and cried into his furry neck. I couldn't breathe. It felt as if I'd been stabbed in the heart. There was a terrible roar in my head that was getting louder and louder.

"Why?"

My love, my life was dead. In one terrible moment, my entire world collapsed. I was paralyzed with anguish. A few minutes ago, I had been happily awaiting Duncan's return, and now... I didn't want to think about the here and now. The pain was too unbearable.

I covered my face and cried as I slid to the floor. Gus tried to comfort me. Poor Gus. Would he understand? I eventually cried myself to sleep. The next day, I only got out of bed to tend to Gus. I had no desire to see anyone. I didn't want to have to think, but that's all I did.

Visions of Duncan and the moments we had shared together crowded my mind. I felt as if I were living a nightmare. Only I knew I'd never awaken from this one.

Gus sensed something was wrong and hardly left my side. When I moved, he did as well. In a way, he was a comfort, as I will be to him when he realizes that Duncan wasn't coming home. We had each other, better than being alone.

That night as I filled his dish with dog food, the phone rang.

"Is this Kendra?" A woman's voice asked sweetly.

"Yes. Who's this?"

"Debbie, Duncan's sister. I didn't have your number or I would have called earlier."

She was probably calling to let me know about the funeral. I had nearly forgotten. In my misery, I didn't think of trying to locate his family.

"Duncan asked me to call you. He's awake now and is aware of his surroundings—"

"What did you say?"

"You can come down and see him since he won't be able to travel for a few days."

"He's alive? The plane crashed. No survivors."

"Kendra, he never made it to the plane, thank God. The taxi cab he was driving in was involved in a six-car collision."

"Please, Debbie, please tell me. Is he going to be all right?" I asked, in a pleading voice with my fingers crossed.

"Yes. He had a bad concussion, and a punctured lung caused by a few broken ribs, but he'll be all right. We didn't know about the accident until the hospital notified us. We also thought he had been on that plane."

"Oh, Debbie, it's a miracle! I can't believe that he's alive." My tears of joy were flowing down my cheeks.

"Take down the address of the hospital and our telephone number. Call me with your plans. I'll come and pick you up at the airport."

"I can't thank you enough for calling."

"I love my brother, too," she replied and we disconnected the call.

I began to dance around the room with the dog trying to keep up with me. "Gus! He's alive, boy. He's alive! Now I need to find someone to watch you."

I called the airlines and purchased a ticket to Atlanta for the following day.

Afterward, I called the veterinarian who tended to Gus when he was sick or needed a vaccination. He was working late and told me to bring the dog right over. He'd board him for me until I got back. Then I called Debbie back with my flight plans. My heart was dancing with joy.

It was difficult for me to sleep a wink that night. I was wound up tighter than a bedspring. I had gone from the pit of despair to a place on top of the world.

Debbie had no problem finding me. Duncan had described me well and we knew what we each were wearing. She was an attractive woman with beautiful black hair that fell gently on her shoulder. She had the same green eyes as her brother and long black lashes. I guessed her to be a few years older than Duncan.

"Have you eaten?"

"We were given a snack and a drink on the plane."

"Then we'll grab something to eat before we go to the hospital," Debbie said.

"I'm not really hungry and would like to go straight to the hospital."

"I know, but my mother prepared a small lunch for you. She can't wait to meet you."

"All right. That's very thoughtful of her and I'd like to meet her as well."

Debbie led me to her car and we drove directly to the house that she and Duncan grew up in. It was small but well-kept. As we walked towards the door, we saw a tall, gray-haired woman standing there waiting for us.

"Hello, Kendra. Come inside. I made you some lunch."

"Thank you. How are you feeling after your bypass?"

"Wonderful! My son is alive, I'm alive. And I just met the woman he wants to marry. I couldn't ask for anything else."

I must have turned bright red because she added, "Oh, he'll be telling you soon."

"You must forgive Ma. She's very outspoken," Debbie said sheepishly.

We went inside and had a lovely lunch. By the time we finished, we had bonded. Duncan was lucky to have such a close family. Even so, I couldn't wait to get to the hospital to see and touch him.

I practically ran into Duncan's room. He was sitting upright in the bed waiting for me. His poor handsome face was all shades of black and blue. I walked over to him with tears forming in my eyes. I was afraid I'd hurt him if I touched him.

A huge grin filled his face. "Come on over here before I jump out of this bed and crawl to you."

"Oh, Duncan. I thought I had lost you."

Tears were streaming down my face. I gently kissed him. When I opened my eyes, he was crying, too.

"I never realized how precious and fragile life can be. In an instant, you can be history."

"I know exactly what you're saying," he added.

"When I get out of here, I'm going to unwrap each day I'm given like a priceless gift and spend them with you. I want to wake up each morning and see your smiling face. And I want your face to be the last thing I see every night."

I only hoped that Duncan was heading in the direction that his mother had mentioned earlier. I loved him more than life itself.

"What I'm trying to say is... Will you marry me, Kendra?"

"Oh, yes! Yes, I will!" I said, taking his hand and kissing it. I feared hurting him by kissing his face.

How beautifully things turned out. Had it not been for Gus, I'd have never met Duncan. That furball turned out to be a golden matchmaker. And now my world couldn't be any brighter.

ALL YOU NEED IS LOVE

Jenny Smith lived alone in a condo located in the residential area of Brook Run in New York. With her job as an ER nurse in a local hospital, she often worked long hours and double shifts leaving little downtime to meet neighbors, let alone, date.

Being an attractive 29-year-old with long red hair and an appealing figure with all the curves in the right places, you'd think Jenny wouldn't lack dates. However, that wasn't the case and she soon came to the realization she wasn't getting any younger. This in turn reminded her that her biological clock for child-bearing was waning as well. She didn't want to end up wishing she'd had children. Instead, she decided to take her fate into her hands and do something about it.

The problem was that Jenny had a difficult time meeting guys to date. She wasn't an outgoing type of person, but couldn't be characterized as a wallflower, either. On the spectrum, Jenny was somewhere in between. She didn't have any real close friends, only acquaintances. And she didn't have the nerve to go to a bar by herself with the hope of meeting a guy. As for the chance of meeting a man in the frozen foods aisle turned out to be nothing more than a mere pipe dream. Not many people shopped during the same crazy hours as Jenny. It would seem that taking control of the reins of her life wasn't going to be a simple matter until the solution came to Jenny in an email ad.

It was an ad from an online dating site called Love Abounds. Its logo was a snapshot of two entwined hearts and the tagline was, "Find love and warm the winter." Jenny read further. "Love Abounds specializes in finding the best matches for all individuals. Give yourself the chance to select that one person you've been waiting for. We know how valuable your time is, so we do all the work for you. So, why not give us a try? You'll be so glad you did!"

Since Jenny was on lunch at the hospital, she couldn't contact the website right away. Besides, she wanted to give it some thought. The right headshot photos and by would have to be sent, as well. If she wasn't too tired when she got home that night, she'd try to write a bio.

The emergency room was hopping that day. Jenny wondered if people would ever stop hurting one another. There were shootings and stabbings, hit and runs, muggings, and all sorts of accidents crowding the waiting room. Everyone waiting to be seen had not gotten by the time Jenny's shift ended at seven. She was exhausted and couldn't wait to go home. On her way to the locker room to grab her things, Jenny was stopped by a young nurse named Allie who had been hired recently.

"Hi! Glad I caught you, Jenny."

"How are things going, Allie? Where did they assign you today?" Jenny asked, knowing Allie could be assigned to any department she was needed.

"The ICU. I'm really getting around lately. I just wanted to ask a favor of you," Allie said.

"What do you need?" Jenny replied, always willing to help a new nurse.

"My cousin, Ted, is coming to stay with me while his apartment is being renovated."

Jenny knew that Allie and her boyfriend, Spencer, were living together and wondered if she was going to like the next thing that Allie said.

"Okay... Where do I fit in?" Jenny asked.

"I didn't want to leave him alone so I thought we could maybe go on a double date if that's all right with you. I'm certain you'll like him."

"When is he coming?" Jenny asked, knowing quite well that most blind dates never, ever work out.

"In a month or so. He's not certain of the exact date, yet. They asked him to relocate for at least a week," Allie replied, looking quite uncomfortable. "I know what people say about blind dates, but Ted is a very nice guy. He's a workaholic, something we can understand with the hours we put in."

"Where does he work?" Jenny asked.

"He's a security analyst and works from home. I really would appreciate this Jenny."

Jenny truly didn't want to say yes, but Allie was a sweet girl. As her brain was trying to come up with a valid excuse not to, she heard herself say, "Okay."

Allie gave her a huge hug. "Thank you, thank you. When I get an actual date, I'll let you know. Believe me, you won't regret this, and I'll owe you one."

Jenny nodded and left thinking to herself, she'd probably regret agreeing to the blind date, but she really couldn't say no, could she? If she thought that, she might even be able to convince herself.

By the time Jenny got home, kicked off her shoes, and had dinner, a thought occurred to her. If she met someone online and hit it off with him, then she'd have the perfect excuse to get out of the blind date. That gave her the impetus to sit down and write the bio. It surely wasn't as difficult as she thought it would be. Going through the pictures on her phone, she selected one and cropped it to fit on the computer screen. Then she sent it off with the bio to Love Abounds. Deep down inside, Jenny didn't have high hopes for online dating. Everyone she asked had either a good story or one that had gone terribly bad. One guy said his date used another person's picture and turned out to be the exact opposite of the description she listed. Actually, Jenny would be surprised if more people didn't do that. The end result was that online dating was certainly a crapshoot.

The next day, though, Jenny was surprised to see five bios and pictures of eligible men in her mailbox. She opened each one and studied the face and the attached blurbs. Able to eliminate three right off the bat, she was left with only two to choose from. The potential dates were pleasant looking and sounded nice. Both were professionals, one was an IT specialist, and the other was a manager of a large department store. Both also sounded personable. All she needed for now, though, was just one of them. The question was which?

Using the age-old method of flipping a coin, Jenny settled on the IT specialist who worked from home. His name was Donald Spillman. Tall at 6'4", he'd tower over Jenny's 5'3" frame, but she'd always liked tall men.

Jenny connected with Donald and they talked for several hours on the phone. He sounded nice enough and suggested that they meet the following Friday at the movies. She agreed and things went smoothly. After the movie, they went for a snack at a local diner and then, like a gentleman, Donald Spillman offered to follow Jenny home.

"Thank you, but it's not necessary, Donald. I'll be fine."

"No, Jenny, I insist. I want to make sure nothing bad happens."

Jenny shrugged. He seemed genuine. "Okay, thank you."

Donald parked his car next to Jenny's when she got home and insisted on following her to her front door. As Jenny began to push the door open, he asked if he could come in and watch a movie with her. Jenny wasn't getting any negative vibes from Donald, so she agreed.

They settled on watching a romantic comedy on the Hallmark station. Jenny uncorked a bottle of wine and they turned on the movie. Within minutes, Jenny began to feel very uncomfortable. He kept trying to tickle her. It wasn't in an inappropriate way, but it did feel off. They weren't in junior high any longer. And if he wasn't doing that, he tried to rub her knee or her shoulder. It became very annoying so she called him out on it.

He became very serious and his reply was over the top. "I'm not touching you."

How can you say that when you are definitely touching me?" Jenny asked. She began to wonder what kind of game he was playing. Finally, Jenny told Donald that she needed to go to the bathroom. As she got off the sofa, he followed her. She closed the door on him and locked it. He remained outside which unnerved her. *What a sicko*, she thought.

Jenny needed to get him to leave but wasn't exactly certain how to accomplish that. She couldn't call the police, because her phone was in her handbag, which was in the kitchen. Finally, an idea came to her that might work. She made gagging sounds as if she was throwing up

"Are you sick, Jenny?" Donald asked through the door.

"Yes. I must've eaten something that didn't agree with me. Please go home now."

"Okay. If you actually have a virus or something, I don't want to get sick."

Jenny put her ear to the door and listened for the opening and closing of the front door. She remained in the bathroom for another 20 minutes in case he was playing with her. When Jenny eventually came out, she found her condo empty. Breathing a sigh of relief, she swore not to accept any more online dates. When Donald Spillman called several days later, she blocked his call and never spoke to him again.

Allie was scheduled to work in the ER two weeks later with Jenny. During lunch the first day, Allie mentioned that her cousin Ted was coming on the weekend. After what happened with Donald, Jenny honestly wanted to beg out of the agreement to double date. She told Allie what happened.

"That's a bummer, Jenny."

"It's a lesson learned. I'm glad nothing more came of it."

"Oh, by the way, I found a picture of my cousin Ted," Allie said as she retrieved it from the pocket of her uniform and handed it to Jenny.

"He's a good-looking guy, Allie. How tall is he?" Jenny asked.

"Pretty tall. I think around 6'3". He's also very nice and has a kind heart, nothing like this Donald creep you told me about."

"I hope so," Jenny said. "I was ready to call this blind date off."

"Don't you dare! You'd be missing out," Ellie replied.

The date was set for that Saturday. They were going out to dinner and then to a live play at a local theater. Jenny figured no matter what, she'd have a nice meal and see a play. Besides, she wasn't going to be alone with this Ted.

On Saturday, when Ted rang her bell, Jenny opened the door and her heart leaped at the sight of him. Holding her wrap and purse, she drank him all in from his magnificent ebony hair, green eyes, dimpled chin, and athletic build, to the tasseled loafers on his feet.

"Here, let me help you with that," Ted said, taking her wrap and placing it around her shoulders.

"Thank you," she said, looking up at him. He was tall. Everything Allie said about him was apparently true.

Ted led her to Spencer's truck and helped to climb inside the back of the cab. Both Allie and Spencer gave her a warm hello. Jenny and Ted talked until he arrived at the restaurant. He was indeed nice, but she reminded herself she thought the same of Donald at the beginning of their date. So, she decided to take things nice and slow. But before long, she realized she was hanging on to Ted's every word.

In the restaurant, they sat side-by-side and she could feel the heat rising from his thigh. She found herself watching his hands as they ate. They were nice hands and she wondered how they'd feel if he touched her Mentally she chastised herself for forgetting she was taking things nice and slow.

The play was a comedy and she liked his laugh. He was deep and contagious. Jenny found she was glad that Ted would be staying with Allie for a week. She wanted to see him again.

They held hands in the theater Jenny liked his touch. She wanted to run her hand down the side of his face. He must've felt something as well because he turned toward her and smiled. That smile warmed every inch of Jenny's body.

At Jenny's door, Ted took her face in his hands and gently kissed her. Jenny hadn't wanted the kiss to end.

"I enjoyed every minute of our date, Jenny. Can we do something tomorrow night?"

"Yes, I'd like that very much, Ted."

He kissed her again. "I've got to go, they're waiting for me. I'll text you."

"Good night, Ted."

Ted smiled and left. Jenny watched him go for a moment before going inside. Leaning against the door, Jenny hugged herself. It was the best date she'd ever been on. Crazy, but she thought she was falling in love with Ted. And why not? He was the embodiment of what Prince Charming should be.

Jenny was amazed at her own behavior. She had wanted to play it nice and cool at a much slower pace with Ted, especially after her date would creepy Donald. And yet, here she was acting like a teenage girl swooning over a cute guy. But she was no longer a 16-year-old. She was a woman who should know her own feelings and accept them. Ted was a nice guy. They clicked. Go with that and build on it. See him again and again if she so desired. There was nothing wrong with any of that.

And so the next night, Ted and Jenny went on a date without Allie and Spencer. They went to a movie and then had pizza afterward. The night was still early so they went back to Jenny's. They played cards and she discovered that Ted was quite lucky at Gin Rummy. It was almost fun to lose because she enjoyed his company so much. They also went through a bottle of wine, as well.

After winning his sixth game, Ted's mood turned serious. "There's something I've got to tell you."

Jenny half expected him to tell her that he was married or something crazy like that and was afraid to hear what he had to say. She didn't want anything to spoil the way she was feeling. There was no way she can get out of hearing it, so she prepared for the worst.

"Jenny, I can't tell you how happy I am that we met. I thought after I divorced my nymphomaniac of a wife, I'd never be able to trust another woman again. You changed all that. It's amazing that in two short dates for me to feel this way, but I know. I can bare my soul and not be afraid you'll tear it to pieces. There is something about you that allows me to feel this way."

"This is so weird. I feel the nearly same way. I want to see where all this leads."

They toasted each other. Following the toast, Jenny said, "I'm done losing card shark."

"Hey, it's just luck."

"How lucky can one person get?" She replied.

Taking her hand in his, he said, "With you, the skies are the limit."

Jenny felt the warmth of his hand and wanted to feel that sensation all over her body. Ted so the look in her eyes and they rose from their chairs together and walked toward her bedroom.

They made sweet love and by the time they were both sated, Jenny knew Ted was the man she wanted to spend the rest of her life with. She knew how crazy that sounded, but it felt so right for her.

Jenny Seward Ted the following night. They discussed what had happened the previous night and were both looking forward to the future. They had Chinese take-out delivered to her condo and had a rematch of Gin Rummy and Jenny even won several games. The TV was on in the background so Ted could watch a football game. He was into sports and played pickleball which explained why he was so fit. When the game ended, no one got up to turn the TV off. They merely continued playing cards.

Then the news came on. The newscaster was talking about a serial killer who had been terrorizing women in Kansas, New Mexico, the Carolinas, New Jersey, and New York. They had finally caught him in New York. He was identified as Donald Spillman, formally of Kansas.

Jenny's face lost all, and she nearly fainted. Ted got up and rushed to her. "Jenny, what's wrong, sweetheart?"

"The serial killer... Donald Spillman..."

"What about him?"

"He was my blind date."

"Oh, Jenny, my God..." Ted said, cradling Jenny in his arms.

Jenny told said all about that horrible night her life crossed paths with Donald Spillman. Because her instincts were spot on, she avoided death but felt sad for those women who hadn't escaped that insane man.

She was a lucky woman. Despite what happened with Donald, she found a wonderful man to spend the rest of her life with.

A CHRISTMAS PRESENT TO REMEMBER

The telephone rang. I'd just finished having lunch with my husband Tom and four-year-old daughter, Laurie.

"I'll get it, Michelle," Tom said, getting up from the table.

He returned two minutes later with a confused look on his face. "It's for you. She says her name is Dottie and that she's *your father's wife*."

I could feel the color draining from my face as my blood turned cold. I had dreaded this moment when my past would come back to haunt me.

"I thought you said your *parents* were *dead*. Do you *know* this woman, Michelle?"

I shook my head. "I promise to explain everything to you after I speak with her."

From the edge in his voice and raised left eyebrow, I could tell Tom was angry I had deceived him. Hopefully, he'd understand my reasons for doing so after hearing my explanation.

"Hello, may I help you?"

"I'm looking for Michelle Trotta."

"That's my maiden name. It's Madsen now."

"My name is Dottie. I'm married to your father, Frank."

Merely hearing his name spoken caused the hair on my neck to rise. "Not to be rude, but why are you calling *me*? I haven't spoken to my father in more than ten years."

"He's had a bad heart attack and doesn't have long to live. I thought you might want to say goodbye."

"I have nothing to say to him."

"You might regret that after he's gone."

I suddenly pictured my father in my mind, fists balled, standing over my mother, cowering in a corner of the kitchen of the house I grew up in. I blinked the vision away.

"He's never forgotten you or ever stopped hoping you'd return. If you change your mind, he's at St. Francis."

I placed the phone back on the cradle. My hands were trembling.

"*Who* was that, Michelle?"

"My father's wife. He's dying."

"For real now? I thought your parents were already dead."

"Actually, only my mother is. As far as I was concerned, so was my father. He was an abusive drunk who'd beat on my mother as if she were a punching bag. One night he hurt her so badly she lost the child she was carrying."

"My God! How old were you when you witnessed this?"

"I was nearly sixteen. My father accompanied her in the ambulance, but she never returned from the hospital."

"She died?"

"Yes. That's what he told me. I could hardly forgive him for that, but at the time I had nowhere to go."

"How horrible, Michelle."

"Dad also told me that he'd stop drinking."

"And did he?" Tom asked.

"Yes, for a short period of time. Then something happened at work and he lost his job. He found solace in the bottle and began to drink again. I wasn't going to stay around while he self-destructed or began to beat on me. So, I took off. My brother had left the year before to join the Navy, so there was no reason for me to stay, just the same."

"And you haven't seen or spoken to your father since?"

"Nope. I never forgave him for hurting Mama and driving her to her death. I've only kept in touch with my brother, Charles. It's funny, you know..."

"What?"

"I once adored my father," I said, as tears filled my eyes. I had no idea whether they were tears from the terrible memories or from the news that he was dying.

Tom drew me close and kissed my head. "Want my opinion?"

I nodded.

"Go see him. You may never get another chance."

"Dottie just said practically the same thing."

"Would you like me to come with you?"

"You don't have to. Besides, I don't know how long I'll be."

"That's okay," Tom replied. "I have some unused vacation time left."

"This trip won't be much of a vacation for you." I cautioned him.

"Nor you. Laurie and I will be there for support."

"I love you, Tom Madsen," I said, kissing him.

He returned the gesture and replied, "And I *love* you, from your size eight shoes to the top of that blonde head of yours."

That made me chuckle. Tom was good at that, always coming out with those corny statements you just had to laugh at. And at that moment, I really needed a good laugh.

I spent most of the next hour on the Internet checking out airline tickets, car rentals, and hotels. When I told our four-year-old daughter about the trip, she became excited and promised to be extra-specially good.

"That means no roller skating in the aisle," Tom said.

"Daddy, puh...leeze!" she said, hands on hips.

Tom and I cracked up laughing. My little mini-me with the golden hair was a pip.

***

I packed our bags, and Tom loaded them into the car. My next-door neighbor, Jane, promised to take in our mail. Laurie had her small overnight bag crammed with crayons, coloring and storybooks, and her favorite doll, Trixie. She had originally wanted to take half her toys, but

I told her we could only afford the seats on one plane. Her response was, "To get real." The things that often came out of her mouth amazed me. Where did she learn these things?

I hated airport security, but it had to be done. We finally boarded the plane and Laurie scrambled into the seat by the window. She couldn't wait to take off.

"What does Florida look like?" she asked.

"It's warm and beautiful. You won't need a coat while we're down there."

Laurie continued to stare out the window, but five minutes into the flight she became bored with the scenery and began to color with Trixie looking on. Sometimes I wished my childhood had turned out more like hers.

I had brought a book to read, but couldn't concentrate. Instead, I rested my head against Tom's shoulder. My thoughts drifted back in time. Ironically, my earliest memories of my childhood were happy ones. My father would come home from work and entertain Charles and me until dinner. Mom loved to collect things, especially antiques. She was forever hauling my brother and me to garage sales. She didn't have the money to buy anything really expensive, but she said it didn't cost to look. She never stopped dreaming and told me one day she'd own a shop. Dad used to laugh at her and accuse her of turning Charles into a sissy. Then things changed. One less-than-happy incident came to mind.

Dad came home from work furious and very drunk. When Mama asked what was wrong, he slapped her hard across her mouth, making it bleed. I'll never forget that shocked look on Mama's face as she held the back of her hand across her bruised mouth. He had never struck her before.

"That's what happens to people who ask questions when they shouldn't," Dad spat at her as he grabbed another beer from the refrigerator and left the kitchen. Mama grabbed us kids and pushed us upstairs, afraid he'd hurt us. He never did, though. Mama had always remained the recipient of his fists.

Dad later begged Mama's forgiveness. He seemed sincere and Mama accepted it. There was peace and quiet in the house once more. Months later, when Dad got drunk, all Hell broke loose. He seemed even more abusive than the last time, and her bruises took longer to heal. But he apologized once more and again, and Mama forgave him. This became their pattern of behavior. Mama would be battered and then he'd beg her forgiveness, ushering in a period of quiet. Then Mama discovered she was pregnant.

Dad became completely irrational, seemingly not wanting the baby. He complained about

going to be waked at all hours by its crying and the smell of dirty diapers. There were times I'd hear them arguing late at night. It all climaxed with one terrible moment that I'll never forget.

Charles had already enlisted in the Navy. Perhaps had he been there, things might have turned out differently. I guess I'll never know. I remember it was a Friday and very hot and humid as summer days in South Florida often were. Dad came home half-tanked, having stopped at a bar with some of his co-workers after work. Mom had just gotten home herself, having stopped at a garage sale on the way to the grocery store. She was just as addicted to them as Dad was to alcohol. Dad was hungry and had expected dinner to be ready. Seeing that it wasn't only made him angry.

An argument broke out. However, when Dad threw an empty bottle of beer at Mama's head, I feared the worst.

"Where have you been, slut? With the daddy of that kid, you got growing inside you?"

"What's wrong with you, Frank? You know there's nobody else."

"Do I?"

"This is the crazy alcohol talking."

"Is it crazy to expect some dinner?"

"I'll have it ready in a moment."

"Not good enough. A working man deserves it to be ready when he comes home."

Mama didn't reply to that and he thought she was ignoring him.

"I'm talking to you, woman!"

"And I'm trying to fix your dinner."

"To Hell with my dinner!" he shouted, sweeping everything from the top of the stove to the floor.

"Why'd you go and do that, Frank?"

"'Cause, you're a lying, cheating whore!"

To have your husband believe that you were having an affair and pregnant with another man's child must have hurt Mama most of all.

I ran back into the kitchen when I heard the splintering of wood. Dad had broken a kitchen chair and was about to pummel Mama with a leg. I grabbed his arm. "No! Don't hurt her!" I screamed.

My father looked into my eyes. His arm was still raised in the air, poised to strike. His eyes refocused and his fury was replaced by the realization that he had done something terrible. He dropped the chair leg and fell to his knees in front of Mama. I looked down at my mother. One eye was closed and blood was streaming from her broken nose and mouth. She was a mess. I could hardly see straight through my tears. Then I saw the blood seeping out from under her. So did my father.

"Michelle, call 911," he said, trying to help my mother up, but she was cowering and backed further into the corner.

I ran back to my mother after I called for help. My father had sobered up somewhat by the time the ambulance came. He accompanied Mama to the hospital and made me stay home. That was the last time I saw Mama. My father came home and told me both the baby and my mother were gone. That was the last time I'd seen my mother.

***

I could feel the oppressive heat rising from the Tarmac as we walked off the plane. The terminal was air-conditioned and more pleasant. I took Laurie to the bathroom before we got our luggage and picked up our car rental.

"Where are we going, Mommy?" she asked excitedly.

"To our hotel and then to sleep. Tomorrow's a big day, young lady."

"What are we doing tomorrow? Is it going to be fun?"

"Most definitely. You and Daddy are going to an amusement park while I go visit somebody who is very sick."

"Do I know them?" Laurie asked.

I shook my head. "Uh-uh."

"Does Daddy?"

"Uh-uh."

"Okay."

I was glad that Tom flew down to Florida with me and as he held me that night, I wondered what I'd say or do when I saw my father after all these years.

***

St. Francis looked the same. I guess hospitals don't change much over time. The walls were the same drab olive I remembered as a kid. I asked the woman at the information desk what room Frank Trotta was in. There was a slight fluttering in the pit of my stomach as I got in the elevator and hit the third-floor button. The feeling intensified as I neared his room. I found it hard to breathe as if my lungs had deflated and stopped working. My palms felt sweaty, and I wiped them against the sides of my slacks. The door was open and the blinds were drawn, further giving a dreary feeling to the discomfort I already felt.

As I slowly entered the room, a tall, woman with fading blonde hair rose from a chair in the corner and took me back outside into the corridor to talk.

"You must be Michelle."

I nodded.

"I'm Dottie."

Still finding my words difficult to find, I said, "I'm glad he wasn't alone." I had no idea why I said that but suddenly found myself wondering if my mother was alone when she died.

"They've got him hooked up to every conceivable machine in there. If he breathes wrong, he sets off alarms."

"How is he?" I asked.

She shook her head. "Not good. He moves in and out of consciousness."

"Will he recognize me?"

"I think so. He was asking for you again. Now that you're here, I think I'll go for a walk and stretch my legs."

I was glad she left. Though I had questions in my mind, I had no desire to talk to her. Actually, I wanted to turn around and flee as an involuntary shiver scurried down my back. The dam holding back all my repressed memories had been breached, and I wasn't certain I could deal with them. Somehow, I found the courage to walk back into the room.

The person lying in the bed bore only a faint resemblance to the robust man my father once had been. His heart condition had obviously taken its toll. As I neared the bed, his eyes fluttered open.

"Hello, Dad."

"Michelle," he whispered in a voice sucked dry. "I knew you'd come."

"How are you feeling?"

He tried to laugh but ended up choking. I helped him sip some water.

"You don't have to talk if it's difficult," I said.

"Got much to tell you. Made too many mistakes. Now's the time to come clean and own up to them." His voice was low and gravelly.

I moved closer to the bed to hear him, figuring it would be all sorts of apologies. He was dying so I decided to be kind and allow him to clear his conscience.

"Go to the house. Get the cigar box from the bottom dresser drawer by my bed." He began to cough again and this time the spasm lasted longer.

"Maybe you should rest a little, Dad," I suggested.

"No. Got to tell you."

"What?"

"About Mary."

"Mom? *What about Mom*? She's dead. You told me she was dead."

I remembered that terrible moment as if it had happened yesterday. Dad was a mess when he came home from the hospital. He was crying and kept saying, "She's gone", over and over again. Mom never came home again and there was no funeral. I'd thought that odd, but Dad said Mom wished to be cremated without any fuss.

I cried so hard that night that I choked choking on my tears. He'd grabbed me by the shoulders and wouldn't let go until I verbally told him that I understood what he'd said.

"In New York. Gallery." His words brought me back to the present.

"What did you say, Dad?" I wasn't certain I heard him correctly.

"New York. Go to New York."

"Who's in New York? he said. "Is Mom in New York?" My mind began to race. What about New York? Was she there? Was he saying that my mother wasn't dead? Had he lied to me? Had he known where she was all this time?

He didn't answer me.

Suddenly all Hell broke loose as the alarms on his monitors went off.

"Dad? Dad, are you alright? What can I do?"

A nurse ran in. "Stand Back! Code Blue!" I backed into a corner as a team rushed in to resuscitate him. Only he was gone. There was nothing anyone could do. He had left me with so many unanswered questions about my mother. I hoped I'd find those answers in the cigar box.

Dottie returned. Her eyes were wet. "I'm sorry," I said to her.

"I knew it was coming. Had lots of time to prepare."

"I guess you were right. He was just hanging on to see me. I'm glad I came."

Dottie gave me an anemic smile. "We'll go back to the house. I know there were things he wanted you to have."

"All right."

"Did you ever get in touch with your brother?" Dottie asked.

"I wrote him, but he's on a ship somewhere in the Pacific. Who knows when he'll get the letter."

"Frank had mentioned he was in the Navy. Spoke about you two nonstop toward the end. He loved you both dearly."

He certainly had a funny way of showing it, I thought to myself.

***

It was an eerie feeling walking into the old house after all this time. I never thought I'd ever see it again. Dottie put on some coffee and I went upstairs in search of the cigar box. I passed my bedroom and looked in. It had been repainted and the quilt on the bed was different, but the furniture remained unchanged. Charles's room wasn't that much different, either. The shelves were still filled with plastic boats and planes. I could almost imagine him sitting at his desk gluing one of his model kits together.

I walked into the master bedroom and closed my eyes. I imagined my mother sitting on the bench in front of the makeup mirror my brother and I had bought her one Christmas. In my mind's eye, she was applying lipstick and laughing at me trying to mimic her. A moment later, the image had faded from my mind and I wiped a stray tear.

The cigar box was exactly where my father said it would be. I removed it from the drawer and opened it. There were photographs of the family taken when Charles and I were small and a few letters from my mother when my dad had been drafted toward the end of the Vietnam War. On the bottom was an unsealed envelope with my name on it. I opened it to find a letter written by my father dated two years ago. I was not prepared to read what he said.

"My Dearest Child,

I have been nothing but a pig-headed, stupid fool who seemed to go out of his way to destroy all those who loved him. For this alone, I surely will burn in Hell. But, if you are reading this now, it means I have passed on. Inside this envelope is a business card. The name on it is your mother's. As far as I know, she still works there. Go see her. Tell her I'm sorry and that I've always loved her, despite those terrible things I said and accused her of. I can't make up for lost time, but I can give you two whatever time is left. Please try and find it in your heart to forgive me and perhaps I'll find some peace. Despite what you think, I've always loved you and Charles. Your mother was a good woman and I treated her abominably.

Basically, that's all I got to say.

Farewell,

Your loving father,

Frank"

The tears were flowing now. What a waste. All that precious time when we could have been a family. I put the letter back into the envelope and put the card into my wallet. I took the cigar box with me downstairs where Dottie was waiting. She'd graciously prepared a small lunch.

"So, you found the box. He was so worried you'd never get it."

"I can see why."

"He was so torn up with the guilt of you not knowing what really happened."

It was hard to describe how I felt at that moment having just learned the truth after so many years. I wasn't certain if I wanted to cry or jump for joy. I know I was very angry at my father for telling such a terrible lie. He robbed a young girl of over ten years of her mother's love.

"I think it's best to have a small funeral, as soon as possible, so you can return home," said Dottie, interrupting my thoughts. She seemed like a nice, level-headed woman. Dad was lucky to have found her.

"Okay. I doubt that he'd want much of a fuss, anyway."

We chattered some more and I thanked her for the lunch. "Dad was lucky to have you. Thank you for taking care of him."

"Frank was mostly a good man. It was the drink that made him crazy."

"Where'd you two meet, anyway?"

"At an AA meeting. We helped each other."

I met Laurie and Tom back at the hotel. Over dinner, I told Tom about my mother being alive and living in Manhattan. Of course, I had to wait until Laurie finished giving me a moment-to-moment replay of her entire day.

"We can go into Manhattan when we get back to New York. It's a weekday, so the gallery will be open."

"Are you certain about this?"

"Of course, I am. If it were me, I'd have been on the plane back to New York, as we speak."

It was moments like this one that reminded me how lucky I was to have such a wonderful guy like Tom.

Dottie was able to get my dad's funeral scheduled for 1:00 pm the following day. It didn't last long and since Dad had been cremated there was no burial. We caught a late afternoon flight and stayed at a motel in Queens. The next morning we intended to drive to Manhattan and see my mother.

"You know, I can't wait to show Laurie the Christmas tree at Rockefeller Center," Tom said sounding like an excited kid himself.

"And many of the store windows have terrific holiday displays."

"Michelle, what street did you say the gallery was on?"

"Fifth Avenue."

"That's great!" he exclaimed.

"Why?"

"I think Central Park is within walking distance. If there's time, I can take Laurie to see the animals in the zoo."

***

I watched as the lights of the New York skyline came into view. No matter where ever I'd been, coming back, and seeing that spectacular sight always gave me goosebumps.

I hadn't slept very well. Knowing I'd soon see my mother again made me jittery with excitement. I wondered how she'd look. Did she still wear her hair the same way? Had the years been kind to her? Questions like these circulated throughout my mind all night until it was eventually time to get up and dress.

We had breakfast and then took the subway to Manhattan. Laurie was excited. She truly loved going to places she'd never been, and this was her first time on a subway. I didn't mention anything about my mother to her, just in case I didn't get to see her or things didn't work out well, but I mentioned to her about going to see a very big Christmas tree.

"Why aren't you coming with us, Mommy?" Laurie asked.

"I have to go speak to somebody. I'll see you soon."

"Promise?" she pleaded.

"Promise. Now go with Daddy and have fun."

"Okay. Ready, Daddy."

I waved goodbye and headed toward the address listed on the card. The Carnivale Galleria was a large store located a block and a half away.

It looked exactly like the kind of place my mother would love to work in. Standing there, I felt suddenly scared. I have no idea why. After all, I'd often dreamed my mother was alive, wishing for this moment. So why did I have cold feet now?

I shook this weird feeling off and walked inside. A doll from the twenties caught my eye, and I stopped to admire it.

"May I help you?" a voice from behind me asked.

I turned around. The years had been kind to her. There was no trace of the damage left by my father's fists. She peered at me more carefully. I was positive she was my mother, for I'd know those loving gray eyes anywhere.

"Michelle, baby, is that you?" she asked.

"Yes, Mama. I'm here."

She opened her arms wide, and I rushed in, shedding those stolen years with each hurried step. She hugged and kissed me, her tears mingling with my own. Then the tears turned to

laughter as she turned me around like she did when I was younger.

"Let me look at you. Why you've become a beautiful woman." Then, lifting my left hand, she added, "And a married one at that."

"Oh, Mama, it's so good to see you. And you have a granddaughter, as well."

"Do I? How old is she? What's her name?"

"My Laurie is four," I said excitedly. "She and Tom, my husband, will be here soon.

"How did you find me?"

"Dad told me."

There was an awkward moment of silence. "How is that man?" she asked.

"He died on Tuesday."

After a moment of reflection, she said, "I was so sorry I had to leave you with him. I didn't know where I was going and had no money to take care of you. I always figured I'd send for you eventually. But then my letters came back unopened. Come, let's sit down and talk."

Mom took me to a small sitting area where there was a carafe of coffee. "Would you like a cup of coffee?"

I nodded and she poured me a cup. I added some creamer and waited until she had poured herself a cup before I picked up the conversation.

"I didn't stay long after you left. When he returned from the hospital, he told me that both you and the baby had died. He promised to stop drinking, and he did for a short time. However, when he started drinking again, I left. I couldn't live with him constantly being drunk. And I feared he'd start beating me."

"So how did you and he finally hook up again?"

"His second wife called me and told me he was dying and had asked to see me. I was a little rude to her and said I didn't care to see him. She said that one day I might regret it, so I went to the hospital."

"Did you meet her?" Mom asked.

"Yes. She turned out to be a very nice person and met Dad at AA. She helped him remain sober. He truly regretted the way he treated you. I think you should read the letter he left."

I opened my purse and took out the letter and handed it to her."

There were tears in her eyes when she finished reading and handed it back to me. "It was the alcohol that made him bad."

Then I changed the subject and asked, "Did you ever find happiness?"

Just then, the chimes over the front door rang and interrupted our conversation. An elderly couple walked in. The woman was dressed in a fur coat and held a Chihuahua wearing his own coat.

"Go help them, Mama. I'll look around." It sounded so weird saying that. I only hoped this wasn't a dream from which I'd soon awake and she'd be gone. I was truly happy to know that my mother had finally fulfilled one of her deepest desires. Finding her here was the affirmation of that. Whereas my dad had looked twenty years older, she looked wonderful, as if she hadn't aged a day. I hadn't detected any gray in her blonde hair. The last time I had seen her, her face looked as if it had gone through a strainer. Not a scar remained. But, had she been happy? I needed to know all about her life during the ten years I lost her.

The elderly couple seemed interested in a particular desk. I was perfectly content to walk around the store. Just as the couple was leaving, I heard the door chimes once more and Laurie came charging in, closely followed by Tom who managed to rein in our active four-year-old before she got into trouble.

"You two look like you certainly had fun."

"It really, really was a big tree, Mommy."

"Glad you liked it, baby," I said. "I'd like you to meet somebody very special."

My daughter turned to look at my mother who was standing there beaming.

"This is Grandma Mary."

"Just like Grandma Erin?"

"Yup. She's my mother. Grandma Erin is Daddy's mother."

"I have two grandmas?"

"Yes," I replied.

"Wowie!" Laurie exclaimed. Then my adorable little girl ran to my mother and took her hand, tugging at it "Hello, Grandma, Mary. I'm Laurie. I'm four."

My mother picked her up and gave her a kiss. "Hello, Laurie. I'm so very happy to meet you."

"Oh, Mom, this is Tom."

"Pleased to meet you, Mom."

"Likewise. We have so much to talk about. Can you stay in the city tonight and have dinner with me?"

"Of course, only we'd like to take you to dinner, Mama." I didn't want to impose on her.

"All right. I will close a little early and take you to a nice restaurant I know you both will like."

"But won't the owner mind if you close too early?" I asked.

"I *am* the owner, sweetheart," she replied.

"But—"

I'll tell you all about that over dinner since it's a long story. "Would you and Tom like to freshen up at my place before we go to dinner?"

"Where do you live?"

"Upstairs."

"It's a converted loft and quite convenient."

"You can say that again," Tom said.

My mother's place was lovely. She even had a piano, which fascinated Laurie. I began to stop Laurie from playing her rendition of a song she recalled from one of her television shows, but my mother allowed her to. "It's been way too quiet up here for such a long time."

I noticed the picture of a silver-haired man on the piano. My mother noticed my gaze.

"That was Hal. He was such a dear man who I lived with since I was still married to your father. Cancer claimed him three years ago. He gave me a job when I needed it most."

My mother sat down on the piano bench next to Laurie. "How would you like to learn to play a real song, honey?"

"Okay, Grandma," Laurie said, beaming.

Then, with the patience of a saint, my mother taught my little girl how to play Chopsticks. Tom and I stood there watching with the pride only parents possess as she nearly got the hang of it.

"Perhaps our Laurie will grow up to be a famous pianist one day," my mother said.

"That may be our cue to take off to the restaurant," I replied.

"Can we get a piano, Daddy?"

"Maybe one day."

"Take this one. Nobody uses it."

"Can we? Oh, please, please, please!" Laurie pleaded.

"We'll discuss it with Grandma later," I said.

We took a taxi to a restaurant several blocks away. "I've eaten here a few times and always found the food good," my mother said as we were seated.

We ordered and began to talk. Ten years is a huge chunk of one's life to fill in. As much as I wanted to know about her life, she also wanted to hear about mine.

"Did you love Daddy?" I asked my mother.

"He was the love of my life."

"He felt the same way about you, Mom. It's a shame he couldn't stop drinking when you were with him."

"The problem was he never truly believed he was an alcoholic. He always blamed everyone else for his failings. I can't tell you how many times he promised to stop drinking. Until he acknowledged he had a drinking problem, I didn't think he'd be able to stay sober for long and I needed time to heal. That last beating was a doozy."

That was certainly true. My father had hurt her so badly that she lost the baby she was carrying, I thought.

"And even if he stayed sober, his possessiveness was nearly as bad. He was a jealous man who always thought I cheated on him. Nothing that I could say or do would convince him that I loved no other man."

"He fell apart after you rejected him and began to drink more and more. That's why I left. I couldn't stay and watch him slowly kill himself," I said.

"Where do you live now?"

"Holbrook. It's out on the Island," I replied. "How did you end up in Manhattan?"

"Believe it or not, someone left a New York Times on the bench in the bus station in Florida. I opened to the want ads and answered one."

"For the Carnivale Galleria?" Tom asked.

"Yes. Hal, of course, was the owner."

"So, you've found some happiness," I said.

"Yes, but not one day ever passed when I didn't pray for you and Charles. I wanted to see you both again before I died. Do you hear from your brother?"

"Not as much as I'd like to. He's out to sea."

"Perhaps he'll be home for Christmas," Tom said.

"Wouldn't that be wonderful? All of us together again," I said. "You *will* spend the holidays with us. Now that I've found you I'm not letting you go."

"You couldn't keep me from my granddaughter if you tried."

It was a wonderful meal, yet if you asked me what I'd eaten, I couldn't tell you. I paid more attention to my mother. For every question asked, two more popped up. After we finished eating, we went back to my mother's place for some more conversation and coffee.

Driving back to Long Island, I thought about how special this Christmas was going to be. Reuniting with my mother was the best present I could ever get and certainly, it would be a Christmas I'd always remember.

The next day I got my mail from my neighbor and found a letter from Charles. I quickly opened it. From what he wrote, it was obvious that he hadn't received my letter about Dad's death. Now I had something wonderful to tell him. I wondered if he'd get the news in time since he was on his way back from the Pacific. The good news was that he said he'd definitely be home for Christmas.

***

The following two weeks were fun-filled and exciting. Mama closed the gallery and came out to spend time with us. Tom was working, but I was able to stay home. Two days before Christmas, a big van pulled into my driveway. It must be a mistake I thought as I watched one man get out and walk to my door.

"Can I help you?" I asked.

"Is this the Madsen residence?" the man asked.

"Yes it is, but I'm not expecting any deliveries."

He broke out into a toothy grin and said, "Guess this one here's a surprise, then."

"Does it say who it's from?" I asked, trying to figure out the mystery.

Behind me, my mother said, "Don't bother the man, Michelle. It's my Christmas present to Laurie."

All at once I knew what it was. "You *didn't*!"

"I most certainly did. Now let the nice man do his job."

"I'm going to have to move things around in here to make room."

"We'll worry about that later," my mother said as Laurie came tearing down the stairs.

"Go sit in the kitchen out of harm's way," Mama told her.

"What's happening, Grandma?"

"You'll see. Have patience, little one."

Laurie went into the kitchen as she was told as the two men carefully guided the piano into the house without hitting the walls.

"Put it over here for now," I said, my mind racing to pick out the best spot in the room.

My mother handed one of the men an envelope. "You did an impeccable job as always."

"Thanks, Mrs. L."

"Thank you, Peter. Oh, don't forget to deliver the Queen Anne desk to the Barry's."

"No, problem. Have a Merry Christmas."

"You, too. Your presents are included."

Both men kissed my mother and were gone.

"I've known those men and their fathers a long time. They're terrific."

"It was amazing how they got the piano in without hitting anything," I replied, truly in awe.

"Can I come out now?" a tiny voice called from the kitchen.

My mother and I laughed. We'd quite forgotten about Laurie left in the kitchen.

"You didn't intend to hide this, did you?" I asked.

Stifling further laughter, she replied, "No. As if it might have been possible."

"Yes," I called back to my child.

Laurie came zooming in and stopped short when she saw the piano. Her eyes lit up as bright as the lights on our tree. "Is *that* for me?"

"It's your Christmas present, Laurie," Mama said.

"Oh, Grandma, you're the greatest," she said, scrambling up to kiss her.

"Promise me you'll only play when your mother says it's okay," my mother told her.

"Why?"

"So you don't disturb anyone," she replied.

Laurie thought about what my mother had said for a moment and replied with her

four-year-old wisdom, "I'll try."

Tom certainly got a surprise when he came home that evening. There was my mother and Laurie sitting side-by-side on the piano bench trying to play a simple tune.

The following evening, we were all sitting in front of the television when there was a knock at the door. Tom got up to answer it.

"I wonder who that could be?" I said to my mother.

A moment or two later, I looked up to see my brother. "Hi, sis. Hey, little one."

"Uncle Charlie!" Laurie shrieked as my mother slid off the sofa.

Charles noticed her and put Laurie down. "Mama?"

They clung to each other for a few minutes. Tears streamed down my mother's face as she kissed Charles over and over again. He began to cry as well. "I thought you were dead... all this time."

Soon the tears were slipping from my eyes watching them. Tom put his arms around my shoulders. "You know something, Michelle? I think this is going to be the most wonderful Christmas."

As Laurie snuggled between us, I looked up at him and replied, "The best."

BENEATH THE VELVET BLUE MOON

"Which star do you want to wish on, Nadine?" Father asked as we leaned against the railing, gazing up at the brilliant star-studded summer sky.

I pointed to the brightest, and we each made a wish.

Sometimes when there were two full moons in one month—Blue Moons—which happened approximately every two and a half years, we made special wishes. All my wishes were special to me, for I always wished for a handsome prince to come and sweep me off my feet. However, I was willing to wait until I grew up.

***

In the summer of my nineteenth year, my wish came true. That was when I met Michael Greene. Michael was everything I'd dreamed my prince would be and we spent those sun-kissed days together. I have to admit, though, we met in a most unconventional way.

On the second day of our vacation at the Jersey Shore, my parents, both English professors at Columbia, were fast at work on the novel they were co-authoring. Basically, that left me pretty much on my own. I grabbed my beach bag and scribbled a note telling them I'd gone to the small beach on the other side of the lake. Chances were, I'd be back before they even read the note, anyway. I only liked to bask, not bake, in the sun. Being a redhead with fair skin, my freckles didn't need new relatives.

I found a nice spot not too far from the water and spread out my blanket. Then I took my book from the bag, stretched out on my stomach, and began to read. Suddenly, out of nowhere, something hit the sand a few inches from my nose.

"What the...!"

"I'm so sorry," a deep male voice said as a hand reached out to help me to a sitting position.

I couldn't actually see him because I had sand in my eyes, not to mention the ton that found its way into the top of my bathing suit.

"Stay right there—don't move. I'll be right back," he said.

I tried to shake some of the sand off me in the few moments he was gone. He returned with wet towels and gently began to wipe the sand off my face. I opened my eyes to find myself gazing into beautiful green eyes.

"Better, huh?" he asked.

"Much." I took the towel from him and wiped the sand from my shoulders and chest. Now that I could see again, I took in the rest of him, from the tussled full head of blue-black hair hanging over his forehead, the straight nose, and dimpled chin, to his muscled arms and chest. In my wildest dreams, I couldn't have conjured up a more handsome guy.

He grabbed the offending missile—a volleyball—and apologized again. "Look, it was an accident. I'm really okay."

Before he could reply, another guy with bronzed skin and windblown hair trotted over. "Hey, you coming back to play?"

My handsome stranger wrinkled his nose and shook his head. "Nah. Play without me," he replied, tossing the ball to the other guy.

"Catch you later," the guy said as he ran off with the ball.

"I'd like to make this up to you. Can I buy you a drink or something to eat at the snack bar?"

"My mother told me never to go off with strangers," I teased.

He smacked his forehead. "Forgive me for not introducing myself. I'm Michael Greene," he said, extending his hand.

I shook his hand and said, "I'm Nadine Stone."

He grinned, his green eyes twinkling. "Now that we're no longer strangers, how about getting something to eat at the snack bar?"

"I really should clean up first."

"No. I don't want to waste a moment."

"I'll only be a few minutes," I protested.

"You might disappear before I can learn everything there is to know about you."

"All right, you win," I said and walked with him to the snack bar, ignoring the annoying sand in my bathing suit.

He bought franks, French fries, and soda for us to eat under the umbrella at one of the small tables. I hadn't realized how hungry I was and quickly took a bite. I must have gotten some mustard on my nose because Michael smiled as he took a napkin and wiped it off. A strange vision passed in front of me of our child asking Michael what he remembers most about me. I can hear the reply now. "Forever wiping off your mother's face. It always seems to get in the way of things."

"Tell me, who are you, Nadine Stone?" he asked, bringing me back to the present where I vowed to be neater.

"Nobody special. I'm starting my sophomore year in college this September at Columbia."

"Have any idea what you want to do when you finish?" he asked before taking another healthy bite of his frank. He must have been just as hungry as I.

"I'm not sure. Maybe teaching, maybe research. What about you?"

"I'm finishing my senior year at Cornell. Architecture's my thing. It was probably the Lincoln Logs my parents bought me when I was a kid."

I chuckled. "You must have designed luxury cabins."

"Not quite. I guess it's in my genes. My dad's an architect, too."

"Well, if genes count, then I'll end up a teacher. Both my parents are English professors. They're hard at work, as we speak, writing the great American novel this summer."

"Together?" he asked, looking skeptical.

I nodded. "They're pretty close."

"I hope they remain that way after the summer is over," Michael said.

I smiled, understanding fully what he meant.

"So, you'll be here the entire summer, Nadine?"

"Yes. How about you?"

"I rented a cabin with two of my buddies from school for the summer. Sort of our last fling before plunging into the real world."

I wanted to know everything there was to know about Michael. As we sat talking, I suddenly became conscious of the rhythm of my heart. It seemed to be beating at a dangerously fast rate. I feared if it beat any faster, it would crash right through me. If he could have this effect on me by only talking, I found myself wondering what would happen if he kissed me. Was there such a thing as love at first sight? I'd never given it much thought until that day, for I'd already fallen in love with Michael Greene.

Being with Michael every day made all ordinary things, like hiking and biking, magical. Of course, my parents weren't completely oblivious to what was going on, nor were they thrilled. My mother felt she needed to caution me. Knowing I was with Michael every day caused her parental radar to go off the screen. Instead of just coming out and saying what she actually meant, she used figures of speech and euphemisms. I found it somewhat amusing that she seemed so uncomfortable.

I was halfway out of the cabin one morning when she stopped me. "Nadine, I'd like to talk with you for a moment."

I turned around and faced her.

"Are you on your way to meet Michael?"

"We're going bike riding around the trails. Why?"

"You'll be careful, of course."

"I'm *always* careful, Mom. And the bike is sturdy."

She had such a look of frustration on her face. "*We're* concerned about you."

"Don't—"

"Seeing someone every day...well..."

"Stop worrying. I'm a *big* girl now."

"*That's* why *we're* worrying."

Obviously, my mother was speaking for my father as well, hence, the use of the pronoun *we*. I knew exactly what they were thinking and worded my reply carefully.

"You and Dad brought me up well. I can tell the difference between what's right and what's wrong. You've instilled in me the smarts needed to make rational choices. So why are you doubting yourselves, now?"

She pursed her lips in thought as she mulled over what I'd said. I'd taken the worrisome wind from her sails and she gave me a less harried, anemic smile. Then I blew her sails into a tailspin when I half-teased, "I love him, Mom. And I'm going to marry him. See ya later."

I left my poor mother standing there wondering whether or not she should chain me to my bed. I might have been kidding with her then, but in my heart, I meant every word. I'd meant what I said about being grown up. I knew what I felt for Michael had to be love. I'd never felt this way about any guy before. The very thought of him had the power to lift my spirits and make my heart soar. I may have spent nearly every summer of my life at the Jersey Shore, but with Michael, I felt as if I were seeing it for the first time. I suddenly became aware of the quiet beauty of the place. I discovered more to do and see than merely hanging out at the beach.

One beautiful star-kissed night in early August, Michael and I walked along the lake holding hands. We stopped by the rail where my father and I had made our wishes when I was a child. A gentle breeze ruffled his hair as he smiled down at me. I smiled back at him. He drew me close and covered my mouth with his. Then he turned to look at the full moon.

"Look, Nadine, it's a Blue Moon."

"My father told me that anything you wished for under a Blue Moon always came true," I said.

"Always?" he asked with the mischievous little smile I found adorable.

"That's what he said."

"Then let's make wishes." His eyes were like emeralds, twinkling in the moonlight.

We closed our eyes and made wishes. I wished to be with Michael forever. Since you couldn't tell anyone your wish or it wouldn't come true, I didn't know what he'd wished for, but by the look on his face, I had a pretty good idea.

"Promise, Nadine...promise me on that Blue Moon that you'll meet me here next year."

"I promise," I said.

Then, under that magnificent moon, we sealed our pledge to meet with a kiss. If I could have put that moment into a bottle and saved it forever, I would have. I had been granted my childhood wish. My handsome prince stood there before me. And no matter what, I knew with all my heart I would always love Michael.

We swapped telephone numbers. I'd keyed his into my cell phone. We'd stay in touch while we both went back to school. And perhaps, if scheduling permitted, get together during the holidays.

That night of promise turned out to be the last night we'd spend together. The next morning, my grandmother called my mother with terrible news. My grandfather had been rushed to the hospital. He'd had a heart attack. I'd hastily said goodbye to Michael. The tears in my eyes were for Michael, but my concern was for my grandfather.

We drove directly to the airport and booked a flight to Arizona. From the airport, we went straight to the hospital. My grandfather was already in the operating room when we got there. We found my grandmother sitting in the waiting room, her eyes red and swollen from crying. My mother tried to comfort her but ended up adding her own tears to the mix. It took another two hours before the doctor came to speak with us.

"Mrs. Carlson, if he gets through the night, he's going to be all right."

A collective sigh of relief could be heard after he gave us this prognosis. He then proceeded to explain what he'd done in the operating room. My grandfather was a feisty old man. Even though Grandpa wasn't out of the woods just yet, we were given hope. I knew that if anyone was going to pull through a quadruple bypass it would be him. We were allowed to peek in on him before we all went to my grandparent's place to spend the night.

The following morning, we returned to the hospital to see him. He was fully awake and though his voice was dry and gravelly, he managed to bark orders to the nurses. Though his skin still bore a gray cast, we knew he was on the mend. And that's what counted.

My parents and I remained in Arizona with my grandmother until my grandfather was able to go home. It wasn't long before he was his usual cantankerous self. He was very political and extremely opinionated. He was forever writing scorching letters to the local newspapers. I guess, no one ever told him it could be dangerous to discuss politics. To tell the truth, when my grandmother had told my mother that Grandpa was in the hospital, I actually thought that somebody had shot him.

We returned to New York in time for the beginning of the new semester. That's about the time I realized I couldn't find my cell phone. For me, it was a category five disaster. It contained every important telephone number—including Michael's.

My father found me in my room ransacking all my bags, dumping everything out, as I frantically searched for my phone.

"What's going on, Nadine? This place looks like it was hit by a bomb," he said.

I must've had a panic-stricken expression on my face when I looked up because his demeanor changed quickly to one of concern.

"What's wrong, honey?"

The pent-up tears began to stream down my cheeks. "I think I lost my cell phone."

"Don't worry. I'll call the carrier and discontinue your service. We'll get you another phone."

"You don't understand..." I whined as more tears welled in my eyes.

"Honey, we'll replace it. Losing your cell phone should be the worst thing that ever happens to you."

"It is."

"You're right, I don't understand," he said, running his fingers through his hair.

"It was my phone book. Michael's number was in it. And now it's gone..."

As if a curtain of uncertainty had just lifted from his eyes, my father took me in his arms and held me as I sobbed on his shoulder. I could tell we were both on the same page now.

"Sweetheart, he'll find a way to get in touch with you."

My father contacted the carrier and let them know I'd lost my phone. I purchased another a few days later. I thought about what my father said. If Michael was going to find a way to contact me, he'd have to be very creative. I now had a new cell phone number and hadn't given him my home number, which is unlisted. My parents didn't want a ton of calls from students.

I tried to get in touch with Michael, but hit a dead end. I was beside myself. How do you meet the man of your dreams only to lose him? The last resort would have to be the summer. Would Michael still keep his promise and come? I never got the chance to find out.

Several weeks before Christmas, my parents were killed instantly in an auto accident caused by a drunk who'd run a red light. We'd started the day, as usual, having breakfast together. Had I known it would be the last time I'd ever see them alive; I would've said all the things I should've told them and held them close. However, I'm no seer and can hardly deal with the present than be able to read the future. Hindsight is grand, isn't it? I've often been told nothing is instant, not even pudding. Well, they were wrong. In an instant I became an orphan. Being an only child, I didn't even have siblings with whom to share my grief. All I had were my grandparents, who flew out to be with me.

It's difficult for me to retell what actually happened from the moment the police came to my door with the news about my mother and father to the days following their funeral because I was in some kind of suspended animation. I knew I wasn't taking their deaths well. In truth, I didn't care. I didn't want to feel. I wanted to believe it was all some stupid nightmare I'd awake from and they'd be still alive.

My grandparents put my house on the market and whisked me back to Arizona with them. During this time, I was a caterpillar living in a cocoon of my own making. My grandparents tried everything they could to bring me out of it, but I resisted. It was easier to sulk and feel sorry for myself. Then I met one of their neighbors, Charlotte White.

Charlotte was much younger than my grandparents. I guessed her age to be around fifty-seven. She had a pleasant, round face, permanently lined from always smiling. The gray streaks in her hair were becoming and she wore her age well. However, it was the inner beauty that made her special. Whether or not our meeting at the pool was planned by my grandmother or merely pure chance, I'll never know. I'm truly glad we had the opportunity to talk.

When my parents' lives were snuffed out like a candle, I had trouble dealing with it because of the way I'd always viewed things. I've never considered myself a deep thinker. Solving the world's problems, I left to my grandfather and others. But I always believed things happened for the best. It's my version of looking at the glass being half-full as opposed to half-empty. I'd tried to find the silver lining or good in everything.

I had a great deal of help in doing so from my father, who was a born optimist if ever there was one.

However, I couldn't find any good in the death of my parents. My entire world had come undone. There was no longer any rhyme or reason to my life. And like my world, I simply came apart at the seams. Until my meeting with Charlotte.

She had lived in Los Angeles, a single mother trying to bring up three kids. Her husband, a construction worker, had died in a freak accident leaving no insurance money. This forced Charlotte to work two jobs in order to keep a roof over her family's head and food on the table. She found it difficult, but had no choice. Her oldest son joined a gang and was killed. The middle child got hooked on drugs, while her youngest was killed in a drive-by shooting. Her world imploded. As she put it, "I didn't just hit bottom, I lived there. I crawled into a bottle of vodka and grew gills."

Looking at her the day we met, I couldn't believe she was the same person she'd just described. She'd had more than her share of tragedy and loss in her life to last three lifetimes and yet she'd pulled herself together and moved on with her life. What was my excuse?

"Don't look so amazed. I found my answer in the Lord. With Jesus' help, I found the strength to stop drinking and help my Jared kick his habit."

No, I didn't find my answer or salvation in religion. Instead, following my conversation with Charlotte, I took a hard look at myself in the mirror. I didn't like what I saw. I'm certain my parents wouldn't have been happy with me, either. They were probably looking down, furious with me for feeling so sorry for myself. Knowing my dad, he'd want me to get on with my life.

I enrolled in the local college and soon decided to become a paralegal. I'd begun a new chapter in my life; one I knew would please my parents. And no, I never forgot Michael. He would always remain in a special part of my heart.

***

I landed a job at a prominent law firm in Phoenix. There were five partners, fifteen lawyers, and three paralegals, including me. At twenty-two, I was the youngest of the paralegals. The other two women were in their late thirties. They took me under their wings, telling me which lawyers to be wary of and which to definitely avoid.

There was one lawyer, in particular, who seemed to be off their radar—Josh Thompson. I met him at my first office Christmas party, which I hadn't wanted to attend at first. Since Michael, I hadn't wanted to date much and found I didn't care one way or the other. Molly, one of the other paralegals, practically twisted my arm.

"Coming to the office Christmas party, Nadine?" she asked during lunch one day.

"No."

"Why not?"

"Don't want to," I replied quickly.

She came back at me immediately. "You never go out. What kind of life is that?"

"Mine. And I like it just fine, thank you very much."

She rolled her eyes at me. "Well, it's about time you started dating again. A pretty girl like you...damn! A nun gets more action."

My face grew hot at her implication, but I managed to say, "I like the way things are."

"How could you? It's as if you're watching the world go by from the other side of the window."

Despite Molly's butting into my personal life, I truly liked her. She'd been a good friend to me from the first day I'd started with Thompson, Brown, St. Charles, Gould, and Woodward. She was always there when I needed help and advice. She also knew about Michael. I'd hoped she'd respect my feelings on the matter of dating and my desire not to get involved with another man.

"Just come to keep me company," she said.

With all she'd done for me, it seemed the least I could do, so I gave in and said, "All right."

"Great." She hugged me, nearly sucking all the air from my lungs. All I wanted was for her to release me so I could breathe again.

***

When Molly and I walked into the employee lounge where the party was being held, the room was already filled with people, buzzing with the cacophony of a dozen different conversations. My gut instinct was to turn around and run. Unfortunately, Molly sensed this and took hold of my arm. "Let's go to the bar and get something to drink. After all, this *is* a party."

We got our drinks and moved off to the side. The room became more crowded and we somehow got separated. This was the last thing I wanted to happen. I backed my way into a corner where I'd feel safer. I didn't mind being alone. However, I soon discovered I wasn't.

A male voice behind me said, "I see you love crowds nearly as much as I do."

I turned to face a tall, pleasant-looking man in a navy-blue pinstriped suit. For a split second, he reminded me of Michael, with his dark good looks. The smiling eyes I looked into were blue, not green.

"Is this your first office Christmas party?" he asked.

I nodded.

"Thought so. I'm Josh Thompson, not to be confused with the partner. Couldn't even get him to adopt me."

I laughed, already liking this man.

"I'm Nadine Stone and probably even lower than you on the food chain."

"Why you have the distinguished look of a lawyer," he replied.

Smiling, I told him I was only a paralegal.

"Don't sell yourself short. Without your work, the cogs of this fine institution wouldn't get oiled."

"Thanks for being nice."

"My fair lady, nice doesn't come into the picture. I was merely being honest. Come, let's refresh our drinks and go sit somewhere and talk. We have a great deal of catching up to do."

Josh and I talked the afternoon away and had dinner together. He was a nice guy and I enjoyed his company. We shared many things in common, especially heartbreak. He was coming out of a relationship that had gone sour after a year and a half. He'd thought she was everything he wanted until he discovered she led a secret life. A sales rep for a large pharmaceutical company, she traveled a great deal. Josh had no idea she had lovers in different states. He discovered this by accident.

"She'd mentioned she had a convention in Las Vegas. Since it was her birthday and I'd never been to Vegas, I decided to go surprise her. Only, I was the one who was surprised."

"What happened?" I asked, leaning closer.

"Well, I was told by the front desk clerk she wasn't in her room. I figured she might've gone out to dinner and decided to have a drink while I waited for her to return. I walked into one of the bars and nearly freaked."

"She was there?"

"Oh, she was there all right. She was in the corner giving some man a lap dance."

"Did you confront her?"

"Not just then. I had a couple of drinks while I tried to calm down. I didn't want to murder her in front of so many witnesses. I waited until they left and followed them up to her room. Now I was certain."

"So, you banged on her door and..."

"Nope. I had a better idea."

This was like a suspense novel. I was hooked and couldn't wait to hear what Josh had done.

"I went home and waited for her to return. She had no idea I knew about Vegas. I'd used my cell phone to take pictures of her with this guy and blew up the pictures. I hung them up over my bed. You should have seen her face when she saw them."

"Just like one of those MasterCard commercials, priceless?"

"Exactly. She couldn't deny it. Spitefully, she told me about the other men. How I didn't strangle her, right then and there, is a miracle."

I knew that woman had hurt Josh badly, for even now, as he retold the story, I could detect pain in his eyes. I found myself telling him about Michael. In a way, we were kindred spirits and became close friends, often having dinner or getting together on the weekends.

In the blink of an eye, two years had flown by. Josh and I grew closer. My grandparents loved him and envisioned us getting married. I loved Josh, but it wasn't the same kind of love I'd had for Michael. It could only be characterized as a comfortable relationship, with no bells ringing or whistles going off. If I married him, I knew I'd never want for anything. He'd be a good husband, faithful and loving. However, as good as it sounded, I felt something was missing.

Josh and I talked about the possibility of marriage, only it was always just that, talk. We didn't go beyond. Perhaps he sensed my hesitancy or was uncertain himself. However, as time wore on, I knew we were heading down that path.

As August approached, Josh found himself wondering where his life was heading and shared these thoughts with me.

"It's time I settled down and began to raise a family. Want to help?"

"Are you asking me to marry you?"

"Yeah, if you'll have me."

I didn't answer right away.

"Are you still unsure?"

"Maybe."

"Not a problem."

I was confused. "What are you getting at?"

"I'm going to be tied up with a pretty big case. Why don't you take a vacation and go cool off somewhere and think about us," he suggested.

I realized it wasn't fair for me to go on indefinitely as we were. Either I wanted to marry him or not. Absence made the heart grow fonder, didn't it? I kissed him goodbye and took a flight back to the Jersey Shore. I hadn't been there in years. The change of scenery would do me good.

I closed the book I'd tried to read and stared out the window. My mind drifted back to that last magical summer I'd spent with Michael. I'd accepted the fact a long time ago that I'd never see him again. And yet, I knew I'd never truly gotten over him any more than I'd forgotten him. So many times during the passing years I thought of him and often wondered where he was and if he'd thought of me. Perhaps going back now I'd be able to close that chapter of my life and be able to marry Josh.

At the airport, I rented a car and drove to the lake. I was lucky to get a cabin for the week. As I drove toward the resort, I noticed changes along the highway. There were more restaurants and strip malls, leaving hardly any open land. The signs of progress, I mused. I rounded the lake. It looked smaller than I'd remembered. The cabins looked older and could've used a fresh coat of paint. Children were playing on the swings at the small playground and several seasonal fishermen were casting their rods from small boats. In my mind's eye, I saw myself riding bikes with Michael around the lake.

Stop it! I scolded myself. I came to think about Josh, not Michael. I went to my cabin and unpacked my things. I could almost hear my parents moving about in the other room. Tears welled in my eyes. I still missed them so much. I blinked away the tears and left the cabin to get something to eat. The manager of the restaurant had gotten older. He still reminded me of Vincent Price, but not in a creepy way. I was surprised when he remembered me. He asked me about my parents and I told him about the accident. I accepted his condolences and sat down at a booth.

I had a grilled cheese sandwich and coffee and read a local newspaper. Families came in for a bite and I wondered if the kids knew how lucky they were to have a family. One thing I'd learned over the last several years was life is so very precious. It's the one commodity you can't replace. I finished my sandwich and returned to the cabin. It had been an early flight and I was exhausted.

After dinner, I strolled to the lake and leaned against the railing—the wishing railing. It was a beautiful night. The sky was blanketed with twinkling stars, reminding me of the times my father and I would wish on a star together. I realized as the full moon rose in the sky that it was a blue one. Dad had insisted all wishes made on a Blue Moon were special and always came true. Even though I no longer believed it, I decided to make a wish, anyway. I'd intended to wish that Josh and I would have a long and happy marriage, but instead of saying Josh, I said Michael. I laughed at my Freudian slip.

Suddenly from behind me, a voice said, "I'd never forgotten that laugh."

My heart began to beat in triple time as I turned to face the man whose infectious smile I'd never forgotten, either.

"Michael?"

"You're more beautiful than I remembered," he said moving closer.

"Am I really seeing you, or have I conjured you up?" I asked, my heart filling with joy.

He chuckled. "I'm actually here, Nadine. I knew if I waited long enough, you'd return, too."

Tears welled in my eyes as I touched his face. He took my hand and brought it to his lips.

"I couldn't reach you during that year and thought I'd see you in the summer..." he began.

As the tears slipped from my eyes, he kissed each and every one of them away.

"My parents were killed, and I lost your phone number. I'm so sorry."

"You're here now. Nothing else matters," he said as he kissed my trembling lips.

When we broke apart, all I could manage to say was, "Oh, Michael, Michael..." before his lips recaptured mine, once more. "I never thought I'd ever see you again," I whispered. "I can't believe you're here with me now."

"I love you, Nadine. I always have and I always will. This time, I'm not letting you get away."

Michael scooped me up into his arms and carried me into his cabin. We made sweet love, and like magic, the years and distance melted away as we were transported back to the golden summer we first met.

I now knew what was missing from the relationship I'd had with Josh. It was the fire and passion I found with Michael. I also knew I would return to Phoenix with a different answer from the one he expected. I didn't want to hurt him, but my life belonged with Michael. It had been ordained. After all, wishes made under the magic of a Blue Moon always came true.

WHEN THE HEART ERRS

Dad couldn't wait to retire so we could move to Florida. He had these fantastic visions of himself playing golf and lounging about in the sun. My mother hated everything about the place, but grinned and bore it just for Dad. We were down there for six years when Dad did the worst possible thing he could do to Mom. He had a massive coronary and keeled over dead putting at the ninth hole. At least he died doing his favorite thing. Now my mother was a martyred widow, grieving for New York almost as much as she grieved for my father.

I had gone back to school for my teaching license and had several months to go before I would graduate from FAU when Dad died. With me having to finish my schooling, Mom felt like a prisoner. "I'm going to die in this horrible place. I'm never going back to New York," she'd often wail, which drove me crazy. How much more guilt could one woman heap on? What made things worse was the fact that my mother refused to drive and hadn't driven in thirty years. This made her dependent on me whenever she needed to go anywhere.

Every day we'd have the same conversation.

"How do you feel, Mom?"

"I'll live."

"I didn't ask you that."

"Okay, get a pencil and sit down."

"For what?"

"To list all my aches and pains."

"Mom, come on, get real."

"I am. You know how much I hate Florida and what it does to my allergies."

"Yes, but when I'm finished with my schooling, we'll be able to move."

"If I live that long."

"Mother!"

She'd purse her lips and look like she was going to cry. No matter how many times she'd do that, it would always break my heart.

"It's not going to be long. I promise."

"Sure, from your mouth into His," she'd say looking up at the ceiling.

When my mother wasn't moaning and groaning about how much she hated Florida, she bemoaned my single status. Why wasn't I married? What would I do when she was gone? Who would be there for me? By the time she was finished, she made me feel guilty that she couldn't die in peace if I remained single.

My problem wasn't that I was grotesque or obese. On the contrary, I was pleasant enough looking with a decent figure. My red hair was my most outstanding feature with my green eyes a close second. I had dated, but nothing ever amounted to anything. All the guys I ever met were losers. If I happened to meet a terrific, good-looking guy who was single, he turned out to be gay. So here I was, tumbling into my late thirties, with not a single marriage prospect in sight. I could live with it if Mom didn't often look at me and burst into tears. That did wonders for my ego.

At least my mother finally stopped trying to fix me up with the sons and nephews of acquaintances. I had to go to great lengths to prove to her how blind dates never worked.

Finally, I graduated and found a teaching position. I figured we'd be able to move a few years after I'd saved some money. However, a short time later, Mom began to act strangely, spending more and more time by herself. My concern forced me to confront her, which I did one night.

"Ma, what are you doing?"

"Nothing."

"Nothing? Why are you sitting in the dark doing nothing? Do your eyes hurt?"

"Why should my eyes hurt?"

"Then why else would you be sitting in the dark?"

"I like the dark."

"Since when? Aren't you the same person who always forgets to shut off all the lights?"

"I've reformed."

"Overnight?"

"Yeah. I took a twelve-step crash course."

"Mom, what's wrong?"

"Nothing's wrong."

"I know you better," I said and noticed she had begun to cry.

I put my arms around her as she had done when I was little and needed consoling. Five minutes later after a good cry, she told me what was troubling her. Lately, she was in constant pain and obviously very frightened. She feared that something terrible was wrong with her, but was much too frightened to go to the doctor. To me, that was silly. I believed that early detection was important, but try convincing a scared seventy-three-year-old.

The next day, I practically had to drag my mother to the doctor. Needless to say, I wanted to run out of there when he told us of his suspicions. A biopsy was set up for the following morning. To my mother, that was as good as a death sentence. Yet, when we were told following the biopsy that she had cancer, she surprised us both and fought valiantly to the end, which was mercifully quick.

Now I *was* an orphan. That was a devastating feeling. I had never been truly alone before and hated the quiet, empty house. I missed my mother's complaining and would have given anything to have her back with me. And then I met a guy—at the funeral home of all places!

He had been paying his respects at the funeral of a friend's father. I had walked out of the chapel for a breath of air and there he was. He turned when he heard me approach.

"Hello," he said. "Fresh air is always a welcome thing. Whose funeral are you attending?"

"My mother's."

"Sorry to hear that."

"Don't be. It was a blessing. She had cancer."

"My friend's father had a massive coronary."

The man was quite handsome. His blond hair was on the longish side and fell neatly on his collar, and his eyes were deep blue. There was a cleft in his chin that definitely added character to his already handsome face. I found it hard to pull my eyes from his face, but one of my relatives was waving to get my attention.

"I'm sorry, but I must go."

"But I don't even know your name."

"It's Sandra Kramer."

"Richard James," he said quickly and took my hand in his. "It was a pleasure meeting you, though I wish it had been at a nicer time and place."

"Me, too."

"Perhaps we'll meet again."

"I'd like that," I said, walking towards my Aunt Francine who was coming to retrieve me.

"Sandra, where have you been? Your Cousin Rose from Texas is here to see you."

I walked back inside the funeral home and was immediately smothered by my second Cousin Rose whom I hadn't seen in years. We were about the same age, yet it would take a few of me to make just one of her. She was about 200 pounds and as wide as she was tall.

After the usual hellos and how much we missed one another, we launched into how neither of us had changed a bit.

"You do know that your mom was one of my favorite relatives? I'm going to miss her so."

Really? How interesting. You hadn't visited or lifted the phone to call her to see how she was doing in a dog's age. I wondered why people were such hypocrites. Funerals seemed to bring them out of the woodwork.

"I'm so glad you could come. Mom would have liked knowing you were here."

Luckily another relative interrupted to pay respects and Cousin Rose moved on. I personally hated funerals. It was up there with how I felt about going to the dentist. And as much as I loved my mother, I couldn't wait for this ordeal to end.

Soon it was time to move on to the cemetery. I got into the limo and closed my eyes. Mom, I am really going to miss you, I silently said.

At the gravesite, the minister recited some psalms, and then the casket was lowered. Watching it disappear into a hole was frightening to me. It meant finality. I wasn't too certain I would be able to deal with that. After everyone had walked away, I remained to say a few last words to my mother. I would probably never know whether or not she heard me, but there was a good chance she did. After all, she always had super ears and heard the slightest sound. I was never able to sneak in the house after my curfew.

As I turned, I found Richard James standing there.

"I was afraid I might not see you again."

"Oh. People are coming back to my house. Would you care to join us?"

"That would be nice. I'll follow your limo."

That's how I met Richard who soon became the focus of my life. I grieved for my mother, but knowing he was there made things easier for me. He was a charming man and Mom would have loved him. In a way, she brought us together. Even in death, she never stopped match-making. I often lifted a glass in her honor.

Since Richard and I were both old enough to understand life and its

implications, neither one of us cared to play games. Richard was well aware that my biological clock was winding down and talked of having a child. We had been dating exclusively for almost six months and saw no reason for a long engagement since we both cared deeply for each other.

My friends often told me how lucky I was to have found a wonderful guy like Richard. However, I already knew that. Therefore, when Richard proposed to me six months from the date we met, I accepted. As he slid the beautiful diamond ring on my finger, he pledged to love me forever.

However, forever is such a long time and our engagement was short-lived. I had no idea that my beautiful dream world would soon come crashing down around me.

About six weeks later, Richard took me to a concert at the Spanish River Park under the stars. We both enjoyed good classical music so this free concert was a delight. During intermission, Richard went to get us some bottled water. When he returned, he seemed visibly upset.

Noticing my concerned gaze, he quickly changed his demeanor, and soon the orchestra and its music transformed the evening into a pleasant one once again. It wasn't until the following evening that I would learn what had taken place during the intermission.

I had begun to prepare some dinner for myself. Richard had called earlier to let me know that he had to go out of town on business and wasn't certain when he'd return. He had mentioned earlier in our relationship that he might have to leave on business trips, so I wasn't concerned.

The early evening news came on. It was the usual stuff and I half-listened to it until I heard Richard's name mentioned. I nearly sliced my thumb off.

Picking up the remote, I made the volume louder. There was an all-points bulletin out on Richard, who also used the names Robert Johnson and Raymond Jordan. He was wanted in four other states for the murder of women whom he had met at funeral homes and subsequently married.

It seems that a woman who had seen his picture and story on America's Most Wanted, a television program, spotted him at a concert and notified the police. There was a little more background stuff on Richard and then

a number to call if he was spotted.

The ramifications of all this hit me hard, leaving me gasping for

breath. I could have ended up dead like the other women! I was a gullible woman who let herself be blinded by this con man in a last-chance attempt to free herself from a fate of loneliness. How pitiful I'd seem to all my friends. And I thought he loved me. Was I so blinded by my own fears? I didn't want to face anyone at this point. I never felt as low and empty. My perfect world was gone in a flash. Now the best I could do was wallow in my own self-pity.

The following day I called in sick. I had absolutely no desire to get out of bed, let alone, leave the house. All I wanted to do was sleep. I'm not exactly certain when I first thought about going to sleep and never waking again, but I decided it was the best way out for me. I'd never have to face anyone ever again. The thought of people pitying me or whispering behind my back was too much to bear.

I don't know why I never threw out all my mother's medicine. Her medicine cabinet was filled with barbiturates and painkillers. I grabbed a bottle and walked into the kitchen. I opened the refrigerator and grabbed the bottle of wine I had originally intended to serve Richard with dinner the other night. As I reached for a glass, I heard a noise from the back of the house. I felt my pulse quicken as I imagined somebody attempting to break into my house. If the person had done his homework, he'd have thought that I was at work. Lately, the entire neighborhood was listening for noises out of the ordinary since the rash of burglaries had begun a month ago. I went back into my bedroom and looked out. There was nobody there. Perhaps it was my imagination.

That's when I saw him standing there.

I nearly jumped off the ground. He laughed at my reaction. I was speechless.

"You surprised me as well. Shouldn't you be at work?"

Finally, I found my voice. "Why are you here, Richard—or whatever name you're calling yourself now?"

"Because you have something I want." His demeanor had completely changed as if he were a total stranger.

The first thing that came to mind was his engagement ring. "If it's your ring, you can have it back," I said ripping it off from my finger as if my skin had been burned. I had forgotten that I was still wearing it.

"Carrie didn't mind me giving it to you," he began to giggle, "but why would she? She was already dead."

He laughed and then said, "All you women are alike. I can almost predict how you will react to everything."

"Why don't you take what you want and go?"

"What's your hurry? Just a few days ago you were willing to give me a lifetime."

"That was before I found out that you—that was before all this."

"Afraid to say, *murderer*?"

I held my breath afraid I might have angered him. The last thing I wanted to do right now was set him off. Funny I should think that now after nearly taking my own life because of him.

"You women made my job so simple, craving love and attention. All I had to do was pretend that I cared and everything was handed to me wrapped in a gift bow, except with you."

Well, he certainly described me well. The one major difference between the others and me was that I survived his *TLC*. Was coming back to kill me worth risking his freedom? No. There was definitely another reason. Why was I standing here debating his reasons for returning when I should be trying to figure out a way to remain alive?

"If that bitch at the concert hadn't recognized me, we'd still be getting married. I'd already have gotten you to buy more life insurance and rewrite your will. A short time later, you'd have met your maker and made me a wealthier man. And all it cost was a little investment in time."

I'm not certain if it was the combination of the irony of the entire episode and my taunt nerves, but I began to laugh. It wasn't a normal laugh, but more of a hysterical one. That definitely irritated him. He liked to be in total control.

"Shut up! You sound like an asinine hyena."

When I didn't stop laughing, he roughly grabbed me by the shoulders and shook me. "Tell me what's so funny, bitch!"

For some unearthly reason, that only added more fuel to my laughter. I couldn't control it. That's when he took the gun out and put it to my head.

"Now shut up and tell me what's so funny or I'll—-"

"What, kill me? "Don't you intend to do that, anyway?"

Then it hit me. He won't kill me until he gets what he came back here for—my money. Only he doesn't know that there isn't any.

"There's no money."

"What?"

"For a smart man, you're acting pretty stupid. What part of that statement don't you understand?"

I have no idea why I was taunting him like this. Maybe I wanted to have a little satisfaction from finding him squirm before he killed me.

"You live in a wealthy area, wear nice clothes. I merely assumed—"

"You know about assuming, don't you? Unfortunately, what money my father had left my mother was used to pay her exorbitant medical bills. There's nothing left. As for me, I'm only a teacher. You know what I make. I'm afraid you risked coming back here for nothing."

I watched the anger build on his face. A vein on the side of his head looked as if it might pop. I can't imagine how I ever felt any love for the man who now stood before me. I also knew that I had very little time left before he sent me to my mother. That scared me most of all, because what was I going to tell her? I was still single.

With his head two inches away from mine, Richard spat, "You mean I wasted time with you?"

"Well, if you weren't marrying me for my charm and wit, yeah, I'm afraid you did."

He backed off and stomped. He was angrier at his miscalculation than he was paying attention to me. I ran into the bathroom and locked the door. It would have been smarter to run out of the room towards the front door, but Richard blocked my way.

The bathroom door was flimsy and would only buy me a few seconds. I had to think fast. I opened the cabinet under the sink. I saw hair spray, body lotion, setting gel, a can of Raid..."

The door broke open. Richard was furious. How dare I try to outsmart him? As he lifted his arm to take aim, I sprayed his face with Raid.

"What the—You blinded me! You bitch!" he screamed, as I ran past him into the arms of a policeman.

"Are you okay, ma'am?"

"Yes, but he isn't."

Richard had stumbled out of the bathroom. The other policeman read him his rights before he cuffed and hauled him off to the police cruiser.

"Boy, am I glad to see you guys," I said to the policeman who stayed behind to ask a few questions for the report.

"It seems that you had everything under control," Patrolman Johnston said, grinning.

"Just don't ask me to do it again. Seriously, who called you?"

"A Mrs. Shein," he said, checking his notes.

I smiled and nodded.

"Do you know her?" he asked.

"Who doesn't? She's the neighborhood nosy body."

"I guess you're glad she happened to be walking her dog and noticed that one of your windows had been jimmied open."

"That's for certain, but...."

"What?"

"I nearly forgot. Richard had a key."

"I guess he chose not to be seen going in your front door," Johnston replied.

After the policemen left, I fully realized the enormity of what had just taken place. Because of sheer luck, I was alive at that moment. I grabbed the glass that I had originally intended to get and collapsed into a chair with a glass of wine. One thought made me smile. Because of me, no other woman will be killed by Richard. Okay, the downside was that I was still single, but hey, there are still some fish left in the sea, aren't there?

ICECAPADE

● Newcastle, Wyoming—Couples are banned from fornicating while standing inside a

walk-in meat freezer

I'm in love with a butcher—plain and simple. Never thought this would happen. Like most girls, I set out to meet and fall in love with a doctor or lawyer. Mama had told me it was just as easy to fall in love with a rich man as it was a poor one. There was one hitch in her advice, though. She neglected to tell me where to find one or how to teach my heart to be more discriminating.

When I first walked into Smith's Meats to buy a pork chop, it was definitely not love at first sight. As Jake Bronson ambled over to wait on me, my eyes were immediately drawn to his apron splattered with dark splotches of dried blood and then the huge, menacingly looking, meat cleaver he was holding in his right hand. It was only on the second glance at this mountain of a man I noticed his thick blue-black head of hair tumbling down to the back of his shirt collar. It was the type of hair you wanted to curl your fingers around. His smiling hazel eyes, thin straight nose and full, pillowed lips rounded out a most attractive looking face. Without the props, he was quite an appealing package.

"Can I get you something?" he asked, putting the meat cleaver down on a cutting board.

As he smiled, I noticed he had two dimples to match the sexy deep cleft in his chin. However, I got the distinct feeling he wasn't looking at my face. Was he checking me out as I him?

"A nice pork chop, please."

"One?" he asked, looking at me as if I'd suddenly grown a second head.

"Yes. I only need one."

It was for my dinner. I was celebrating the sale of an article I'd written for a magazine. Living alone, I rarely cooked.

"No one buys only one," he replied with an air of authority.

Says who? Anger crept into my voice as I replied, "Well, I do. Now, will you please give me my pork chop?"

He answered me with a shrug, pulled out a tray and selected a chop. However, from the way he ripped off a sheet of freezer paper and slapped the chop down, I knew he was steaming. I watched him deftly wrap it. As he handed it to me he asked, "Anything else, Ma'am?"

"No. That's all, thank you," I replied as I began to walk away, still annoyed with the man's rudeness and roving eyes.

"You know, you shouldn't eat alone," he called after me.

That did it! Who the devil did he think he was? I stormed back over to the counter to confront him. My personal life was just that—personal.

"And what's it to you?" I asked.

He gave me that stupid shrug again. How I hated when he did that.

"Just figured a pretty gal like you should have company."

"That's none of *your* concern."

"Maybe. There are lots of things I care about," he said, staring at my chest again.

He certainly wasn't winning points with me. Too bad, I thought. After all, he was quite a

good-looking guy. Busy with my own thoughts, I missed the last thing he'd said.

"Well, how do you intend to do it?" he asked.

What the devil was he talking about now? "Do what?"

"Cook the chop?"

Now I looked at him as if he were crazy. Why did he care how I cooked the damn thing? Next he'll ask me how I intend to chew it. I threw back my head and placed my hands on my hips.

"Put it in a pan and fry it," I answered defiantly.

Suddenly his face darkened like a winter's sky and his voice, cold and lashing. "Are you nuts, lady? How can you take a beautiful piece of meat and murder it?"

"What do you know? You can cook it better?" I challenged, leaning over the counter.

"You bet, I do," he replied with more than a hint of contempt.

His tone aroused and infuriated me. I wasn't going to let him have the last word. I chortled. "What does a man know about cooking?"

"A great deal...and I can prove it!" His glare met mine.

"Sure you can," I taunted him.

"You don't believe me? I'll come home with you tonight and show you how to cook pork

chops properly," he replied to my challenge.

"Then you'd better bring another to replace this one when you ruin it," I added.

All at once the realization of what had just taken place hit me. I'd just invited a total stranger to my apartment to cook dinner for me. How in the world did I allow it to happen? Before I could open my mouth to switch feet, he sealed the deal.

"I'll be closing in forty minutes. Give me your address," he said, handing me a pencil and a small, green order pad to write it down.

I felt as if I'd signed my own death sentence. The way he handled that meat cleaver, he

could be a murderer. After all, he *was* a butcher, wasn't he?

I sped home as if I were possessed, not knowing what to do first. Should I straighten the apartment, shower, make certain the oven is working? *Hold it!* I scolded myself. Listen to what you're saying. Just because he's handsome and seemed to be interested in you, you're tripping over your tongue. You're acting like an adolescent. Pull yourself together, girl. He'll be here soon. And for heaven's sake, don't act as if you haven't gone out on a date for ages.

By the time the handsome butcher had knocked on my door, I'd been able to clear the old newspapers off the extra kitchen chair and put away the dishes in the drying rack. I would never add good housekeeping to my resume. It was even further below my cooking skills.

He walked inside carrying a package of meat, a bottle of wine and a single long-stemmed red rose. I was confused. First, he chastises me for the premeditated murder of a pork chop and then he comes waltzing in as if he were going to wine and dine me and. Who *was* this guy?

There was an embarrassed half-smile plastered on the man's face as he said, "Hello...?"

"MaryAnn. My name is MaryAnn Hedges."

The red hue quickly faded from his face and his smile became whole again as he replied,

"I'm Jake Bronson."

"Come on in, Jake. Sorry, it's not much," I apologized, suddenly ashamed of my studio apartment with its second-hand furnishings.Unfortunately, big bucks don't come with my job description at the bank.

"It kinda looks like mine," he said, walking towards the small wrought–iron kitchen table where he put the meat and wine down.

"I'll take that," I said, taking the rose and placing it into a half-filled water glass, making a mental note to invest in a vase.

"If we're gonna eat some time tonight, I'd better start cooking." Jake said.

"Can I help?"

"You can get me the following stuff: breadcrumbs, salt, pepper, cornstarch, garlic, oil tomatoes—"

"Whoa! Slow down. You lost me."

"Sorry. I'll find the things I need myself. You set the table—or better still—make a salad. You *do* have fresh vegetables in the frig, don't you?"

Luckily, I did. For some reason I felt like having a salad yesterday and had stopped at the market on the way home from work.

I nodded, feeling good about having done something right. Even if it was by accident. Jake quickly busied himself gathering the ingredients he needed. He looked like he knew his way around a kitchen. This aroused my curiosity as well as something else I couldn't quite define yet.

Ripping apart the lettuce, I asked, "Where did you learn to cook?"

He continued to bread the chops without turning to face me and said, "My mother died when I was thirteen. Being the oldest of four kids and Dad working two jobs, I had no choice."

I wondered what other things he could do as well.

It wasn't long before the kitchen smelled wonderful. A home cooked meal was another thing I'd not had in ages.

I set the table. There was little room to put anything in addition to the plates, glasses, and silverware. Even so, I put the rose in the center. This space problem never came up before. I usually ate dinner at the sink out of the pot.

I watched Jake as he began to put everything on platters. He was such an attractive man,

one I'd like to get to know better. Or could my loneliness be talking. It had been some time

since I'd had a meaningful relationship.

"Have you a corkscrew?" Jake asked, interrupting my thoughts.

"Yes. I'll get it," I replied, walking towards my so-called junk drawer where I kept miscellaneous items. The only problem was once you took something out; you could never close the drawer again. This time, I was lucky and only struggled a few moments before I succeeded.

I handed it to him and he popped the cork, shooting it clear across the room. We both broke into laughter before I retrieved it.

We began to eat. The man could cook and I was impressed. All the men I'd known in my life, including my dad, only went into the kitchen to eat. Cooking was alien. Only women and wusses cooked.

"Jake, this is delicious. This is by far the best pork chop I've ever eaten."

Jake broke into a huge grin. "You ought to see what else I can do—"

"Shouldn't we wait for the third date?" I replied, trying to repress a smile.

He began to laugh. "I was referring to my special chicken dish."

"Of course you were."

After breaking the ice, we reached the part where we talked about ourselves and tried to learn as much as we could about each other. I'd rather hear all about him, though. Not having what you'd call a sterling childhood, I tried to forget it every existed, let alone discuss it. My dad was a gambler who lost his job, the household savings and insurance. Mom took me and left him, forced to struggle to keep a roof over our heads and food on the table.

Jake stayed until 11:30. We'd had such a good time, we made a real date for the following Saturday. I went to bed wondering if he was the one man put on this earth for me. From what I could see at this point, he certainly met all the criteria.

***

The week blew by. Jake took me to his favorite steak house for dinner. Afterwards we went to play pool. He had brought his own cue stick and knew how to use it.

"My grandfather taught me how to play when I was seven."

"I don't want to ruin your game. I'll watch you play—"

"Don't be silly. It's fun. Come here. I'll show you."

I took the cue and he put his arms around me to guide the shot. Being so close to him, his aftershave intoxicated me and my skin tingled where he touched me. I wanted to forget the game and lose myself in him.

"It's all in the angles," he was telling me, but I found it so hard to concentrate.

He made it seem so easy. No matter how bad I was, he patiently encouraged me. I was beginning to have fun when his cell phone rang. He glanced at the caller ID and his smile was quickly replaced by a look of apprehension.

"Gotta take this he said," walking out of earshot.

As I attempted to hit the seven ball into the pocket, I watched him gesture as he spoke.

Whoever had called him was not on his Christmas list. The call was quick, and he returned in a soured mood.

"Sorry," he said.

I didn't want to pry, but I was concerned. "Are you okay, Jake?"

"Couldn't be better," he spat. "Let's get out of here. I need some air."

Without another word, he put his cue stick back into its case and we left. He took me home.

As he walked me to my apartment, I asked, "Would you like to come in for coffee or wine?"

He shook his head. "I have to get up early tomorrow and open up."

"Maybe next time."

"Sure," he said.

He began to walk away, leaving me disappointed. Then, as if he were reading my mind, Jake walked back and kissed me. He had the most kissable lips and sent me spinning. Still reeling, I heard him say, "I'll call you," before he left.

I chalked up his change in behavior to having to cover another guy's shift. No one ever likes to go in on their day off. I should know. I often had to do it at the bank.

***

Jake and I continued to date and I had fallen in love with him. In my heart, I knew he was the guy I wanted to share my life with—until I discovered another side of him.

We were having a ball at the State Fair acting like a pair of kids when his cell phone rang. Jake looked upset, reminding me of the night in the pool hall. However, this time, I heard him reply. "Okay, okay, I told you…I'll have the money by next Wednesday."

My stomach knotted. Jake had either borrowed money from a loan shark, or, worse, lost a bet. I'd had my fill of gamblers and swore I'd never get involved with one.

"What's wrong, Jake?"

"This doesn't concern you."

"Hey, I love you. What kind of future could we have together if you don't trust me?" I asked, half-wanting not to know.

"I bet on the ponies. It was a sure thing."

"My father used to tell my mother the same thing. You know what's definite—?"

"I know. Death and taxes. I knew I shouldn't have told you."

I took his hand. "Listen to me, Jake. Gambling destroyed my family and killed my dad. If you win one bet, you lose three more. Promise me you'll stop," I begged him.

"I don't know if I can," he replied.

"If you don't, I can't be with you."

His eyes pleaded with me to take my words back, but I couldn't.

"I'll help you, Jake, I said. "Only, you've got to swear you'll stop."

He grabbed me by my shoulders and covered my mouth with his before he whispered, "I swear."

I helped Jake raise the money to pay his bookie and he kept his word to stop betting. Had he not, leaving him would have been the most difficult thing I'd ever done.

***

Jake and I were fast asleep when the annoying ringing of his phone awakened us. After a night of love making, I'd welcomed sleep. Groggily, I raised my head to see Jake answer.

"Do you know what time it is?" he growled into the receiver. "So, what? 5:00 am is no

time to call anyone. Jerry's always sick. What if I don't want to come in? Okay! I

heard you the first time. I'll be there," he said, slamming the receiver down hard enough to break it.

"What's wrong, Jake?" I asked, rubbing his back.

"Go back to sleep, MaryAnn," he said as he rose from the bed. Just seeing his wickedly beautiful body began to stir my juices.

"Where are you going at this hour?"

"To take a shower. Jerry's called in sick. I've gotta take his damn shift again."

This was the third time this month. We'd made plans to go to a barbecue today at his brother's house. I'd been looking forward to going. Jake turned back. "I'm sorry about the barbecue."

"Not your fault."

"I'll bring home a nice London broil," he replied, probably hoping to appease me.

I rolled over and closed my eyes. I never heard him leave.

***

When I came out of the shower, I noticed the red light on the answering machine blinking.

Thinking I'd missed Jake's call, I played back the message.

"Bronson! No more stalling. I want my money today!" the raspy voice of a heavy smoker snarled. "I'm sending Iggy to the store. If you don't have it, I don't have to tell ya what's gonna happen..." This message was followed by a choking laugh before the connection was finally broken.

"Damn you, Jake!" I said aloud. "You promised to stop gambling."

Then it hit me. I had to warn him. I grabbed the phone and called the store. It was busy.

I tried his cell number and nearly lost it when it went directly into his voice mail. There was no time to waste. I threw on some sweats and drove to the store, praying I'd get there before this Iggy person. As angry as I was with Jake for breaking his promise and betting again, I couldn't bear to see him hurt by some loan shark's enforcer. I'll never forget how my father looked. I envisioned Iggy to be a gorilla of a man who loved his Louisville slugger more than his own mother.

As I drove, every passing second felt like a hand at my throat tightening its grip,

making each breath more and more difficult. By the time I parked the car and rushed into the

store, I was breathless.

I startled Jake and the elderly woman he was waiting on. They both looked at me as if I were some lunatic. She paid for her meat and left there as quickly as her arthritic legs could carry her, not waiting for her change.

"What's wrong, MaryAnn? You look like you've seen a ghost." Jake said, eyebrows still raised in surprise.

Forcing myself to breathe, I spoke in gasps. "Iggy's on his way here to collect money."

The color drained from Jake's face. "Iggy? How do *you* know?"

"Your loan shark called the apartment. You've been betting again. How could—"

The slamming of a car door interrupted me. Jake came around the counter and grabbed my hand. With me in tow, he headed for the walk-in freezer. Just as the heavy door closed behind us, we heard the bells over the front door tinkle. I prayed it was only a customer.

Jake held a finger to his lips. I watched as he grabbed a broom standing by the door and wedged it into the handle. Then he pushed me further into the room. The overwhelming smell nearly made me retch as I knocked into disgusting animal carcasses hanging from meat hooks. I could swear the pigs were staring at me with their lifeless, black beady eyes. The sawdust on the floor stuck to the soles of my sneakers. It felt like the Arctic in there and I began to shiver from the cold. Jake put his arm around me. I was miserable, but I knew the alternative was worse.

Suddenly we heard pounding on the door as loud as thunder. Jake drew me closer.

"Bronson! I know you're in there. Come out now and I won't break every bone."

"Nice guy," I whispered.

The lack of color on Jake's face wasn't just from the cold. Nor was the worry in his eyes. He was as frightened as I was.

The pounding grew louder and more intense. Iggy was probably getting frustrated. As he

banged on the door and tugged at the latch, he made threats and screamed obscenities. "You're a dead man, Bronson! You hear me? A dead man!"

Now I truly feared for Jake's life. What if Iggy was able to get the door of the freezer open? He didn't sound like the kind of guy who'd listen to reason. An involuntary shiver shook my body.

"I'm so sorry, baby," he whispered.

"Why'd you do it? You promised."

"It was a sure thing. Honest. I swear it."

"Nothing but death and taxes—and Iggy—are sure things."

"But I needed the money."

"What was so important?" I asked him without hiding the anger I felt.

"I...I wanted to buy something," he replied, looking away.

"Nothing could be so important you'd put your life in danger."

"The truth is...I wanted to buy a ring for you."

I looked at him. Tears began to fill my eyes. I felt speechless. "Oh. Jake," I began, but I couldn't speak. He gently touched my face and kissed the top of my head. With tears streaming down my face, I looked up at him. My anger had abated. He did it because of me—because he loved me. I loved him, too. And now I feared I'd lose him because of some creature named Iggy.

He wiped the tears from my face and gave me a smile before he covered my mouth with his. It was a gentle kiss. We kissed again, but this one became more passionate. Soon the beating of our hearts drowned out Iggy. We sank to the floor, oblivious to the sawdust covering it. Our passion had become bewitching, allowing us to forget our present surroundings and the danger we were in. All we saw was each other. The articles of clothing separating our newly heated bodies from one another were quickly discarded as we made frantic love amongst the hanging carcasses in the freezer.

We were way too busy defrosting the freezer to notice the pounding had stopped. Only when the door of the freezer was removed from its squeaky hinges, did it get our attention. Suddenly, we looked up and found ourselves surrounded by Jake's boss, Alton Smith, two gawking policemen and three smirking firemen. I grabbed my jacket in a feeble attempt to cover up. To say I was mortified would be an understatement.

"What the hell are you two doing? The shop is trashed," Smith said, glaring at us with such anger, I quickly froze again. "I'm holding you responsible, Jake."

"I'll make good," Jake said.

"The hell you *will*. Why are you in here in the first place?" Smith asked.

"I'm afraid we're all going to have to take this downtown," one of the policemen said,
interrupting.

"What for?" Smith asked. "I'm only pressing charges against that lunatic you have out there."

"I'm afraid *this* is an entirely different issue," the cop answered.

"What issue?" both Smith and Jake asked, nearly in unison.

"I believe they've broken the law, penal code 1148. It concerns fornicating in a freezer."

"You've got to be kidding," Jake said.

"I assure you, sir, I am *not* joking. Now if you and the lady will get dressed..."

"Would you please give us some privacy?" I asked.

The other cop who had remained quiet until now said, "What's there left to see?"

I think Jake's clenched fists and murderous look helped the other men see things differently. After they walked out, we began to dress quickly.

"I don't believe this, Jake."

"And I suppose you think I do?" he replied curtly.

"It's no use for us to argue. We're in this together."

"I'm sorry, hon. Things haven't been going quite right today."

"You've noticed," I replied, brushing as much sawdust off of me as possible. It was starting to get itchy in places I never thought possible.

"Let's go, you two!" a voice called in to us.

"No matter what, MaryAnn, you've got to believe how sorry I am about all this," he said, gesturing with his arms.

Remembering the reason why he needed the money in the first place, I softened my tone and gently touched the side of his face. "I know."

He took my hand and we walked out together. No matter what happened next, we'd face it

as a team.

***

We were hauled in front of a judge. The name plate sitting on his huge wooden desk read Thomas A. Poole. The man looked as if he'd been roused from his bed. Thin as a rail, sagging skin the color of sandpaper, the bags under his nearly colorless eyes were more like buckets. His hair, white as freshly fallen snow, stood on ends in places, looking as if it were cut by a buzz saw. He had a scowl on his face and a bulbous nose that reminded me of a well-used road map. A set of hanging jowls completed the picture likening him to a bloodhound. Something told me we were in for it, so I prepared for the worst.

Poole waved a long, arthritic-looking, bony finger at the both of us. "Shame on you! You've broken the law. What do you have to say for yourselves?"

"It's my fault, Your Honor—" Jake began to say, but Poole shut him down.

"Who gave you permission to speak—?"

"But Your Honor—" Jake protested.

"It was a rhetorical question, young man. You are to speak *only* when I tell you to."

Oh, boy, I thought. *We've got ourselves a real winner.*

"You are accused of fornicating while standing inside a store's meat freezer. What say ye?"

Neither one of us uttered a sound. The color of the Judge's face began to redden. "I asked you a question," he spat.

"Does that mean you want us to speak?" Jake asked.

"Are you deaf or just plain stupid?" Poole replied.

"We're not guilty, Your Honor," I said.

As Poole's face now took on a purplish hue, I felt the eyes of the two policemen who had escorted us into court, bore into me. Jake looked at me, eyebrows raised. I put a finger to my lips. I wanted him to trust me. I knew where I was going with this.

"What did you just say, young lady?" Poole asked, fixing his rheumy eyes on me.

I swallowed hard, repeating what I'd just said.

Poole looked so angry I thought the large, throbbing, blue blood vessel on the side of his wizened head would explode. Instead, he banged his gavel a few times. "Are you daft, as well? You were caught with your knickers down and you stand there telling me you're innocent...I should throw the book at the both of you."

"Your Honor, Sir, according to the penal code, a couple is banned from having sex while standing. Jake and I...we...weren't standing. We were lying on the floor."

"Officer Stewart, how did you find them?" Poole asked.

"On the floor, Your Honor," he said I nearly a whisper.

"Speak up!" Poole demanded.

The officer repeated his statement. Visible beads of sweat had formed along his high forehead. The Judge looked like he was going to boil him in oil. Instead, Poole made a sound that sounded like a low growl.

"As far as I'm concerned, you two are guilty as sin. Intercourse is intercourse in my book whether you're standing or not. However, in our bleeding, liberal-livered society, some ambulance chasing moron of a lawyer will get you off. Get out of my court," he said and slammed the gavel down as hard as he could.

Jake hugged me and together we high-tailed it out of there. All we heard as we fled was

Poole ordering the two policemen to remain. I had a feeling they both were in big trouble.

"Baby, you were magnificent!" Jake said, kissing me.

"We're not out of the frying pan, yet," I said seeing Anton Smith walking towards us.

"Huh, what do you mean?" he asked.

Before I had a chance to answer, Smith stood before us.

"Look, before you fire me, I intend to work, even overtime, in order to repay you for the damage," Jake said.

Instead of ragging on Jake, the man broke into a huge smile and clapped him on the back.

Now I was certain the entire world had gone mad.

"You're not angry?" Jake asked, obviously just as bewildered as I was.

"Of course not," Smith replied.

"I don't understand," Jake replied, definitely wondering about his sudden change of heart.

"Thanks to your little run in with your loan shark, I can now renovate. The insurance company has agreed to pay for everything. You're off the hook, man."

Now if only Jake could get squared away with the loan shark. A ray of hope entered my thoughts. If only Iggy was promised a deal and ratted out his boss... Whatever, it didn't matter. Jake wasn't alone in this. We'd find some way to raise the money together. Afterwards, I'd delete the loan shark's number from Jake's cell phone, permanently.

We walked out of the courthouse arm-in-arm, a great deal happier than when we first entered.

"Hungry?" Jake asked.

"Starved," was my reply.

"I know just the thing," he said pulling me towards the hotdog stand. "Tell the man what
you'd like."

I ordered two dogs with everything on them. Jake got the same. We sat together on a bench biting into oozing hot dogs, getting more mustard and chili on our faces than in our mouths. To tell the truth, I was having the time of my life. After they were completely devoured and we'd made an attempt to clean ourselves up, Jake reached into his pocket and pulled out a small jewelry box. He handed it to me and said, "Open it."

My hands trembled. Inside I found a beautiful diamond ring.

"Will you marry me?"

"You know I will," I replied as he slipped the ring on my finger.

"I guess it was just one of those *sure* things," he said, grinning.

Then he took me in his arms and we kissed. A cranky voice interrupted us. "You two are incorrigible. I should have slapped both your asses in jail when I had the chance." The judge was standing there before us shaking his head.

Some Other Stories from Candy Caine

For Your Love
Justify My Love
A Bridge to Love
Dancing for Dollars
Forever in My Heart
Honor Most Profane
Softly, As I leave You
Save the Last dance for Me
No Strings Attached
Heated Pleasures, Peek into the World of Candy Caine
At First Sight
Because of You
Flavor of the Week
It's Love that Really Counts
For the Love of Money
Crazy Love
Through the Keyhole
Forever Yours
Overboard
That Summer

ABOUT THE AUTHOR

Whether she's writing red-hot interracial or less edgy contemporary romance, Candy Caine believes in living life to its fullest with her best friend and husband, Robert.

www.ingramcontent.com/pod-product-compliance
Lightning Source LLC
Chambersburg PA
CBHW022207150726
47992CB00002B/1003